IMAGINE:
The Golden Starpearl
by

CHARLIE BATT

IMAGINE Series: Book 3

About Charlie

Charlie Batt lives on the east coast of Australia. She is a very talented seventeen-year-old who is on the autism spectrum. She loves storytelling and drawing and has put her talents into writing the Imagine series.

You can find her at www.charliebatt.com

Other books

IMAGINE

Book 1: Imagine: a Wild Civilisation
Book 2 - parts 1, 2 and 3: Imagine: the Long Winter
Book 4: Imagine: High Worlds
Book 5: Imagine: A Dark Underworld

Book 6: Imagine: The Rise of the Mindatar

COLOUR CODES OF CHARACTERS

PINK - Charlie

PINK and TEAL - Jayjay

BLUE - Sandy

LIGHT BLUE - Barbara

RED, PINK and BLUE - Atom

LIGHT RED - Chuckboi

DARK BLUE - Bucky

ORANGE - Violet

BRIGHT BLUE - Tar

GREEN - Stephenie

DARK GREEN - Eric

TURQUOISE and DARK BLUE - Jasper

HOT PINK - Pearl

GOLD - Orla, the Mother of Gold (*psychic*)

TURQUOISE - Kira

BRIGHT YELLOW - Lulu the Golden Starpearl
(*psychic*)

Note:(There are more different colours that are not included in the Colour Codes of Characters page. Those excluded colour codes represent different types of sea life and some other land characters in this book.)

Prologue

This is the third story that I will tell you.

In this story you are about to read, you are about to discover another world full of coral, tentacles, scales, shells, sand and things that swish with the currents: the ocean.

This underwater world supports so many mysterious sea creatures and places that feel alien.

But unlike all aquatic species, another relative of the Singanoid Race is found living in the sea called the Mersinganoids. These two-coloured, beautiful aquatic relatives spend most of their lives underwater and avoid the sunlight. Like a vampire out in the sun, the body will burn, scales will fall off, and they will dry out, eventually becoming a lifeless body of what was once a living thing.

That is a terrible way to die for those poor souls. But that's why they avoid the sunlight or stumbling into anywhere too hot where their flesh will burn.

Aside from that, like the first two members of the Singanoid Race, the Mersinganoids have beliefs. One is about me, but the other is a belief in a giant ancient Kraken known as the Mother of Gold. This mother, in the Summertime, would swim out from the darkness of the deep to the light of day every three years after sleeping on an ancient giant tree called the Deep Spirit

Tree. This tree is the Mother of Gold's home and a sanctuary for the spirits of aquatic creatures, even Mersinganoids, who passed on to roam peacefully in their afterlife until they would one day reincarnate.

The Mother of Gold, when she rises to the surface, heads for an island known as Mersinganoid Cove.

Mersinganoid Cove is the home of all Mersinganoids to sleep, sing, survive and keep their home healthy. The island's surface is rich in Violet Palm Trees with mineral and salt-rich mud that surrounds a massive deep cenote, where the Mother of Gold enters through a giant tunnel.

Before she arrives at Mersinganoid Cove, she passes through a place called the Deep Blue, where the area below shows only an inky darkness but lights up with small, sparkling lights called Sea Stars.

The Deep Blue is also where winding and twisting currents are used as travelling passages, one leading to her Deep Spirit Tree.

In Mersinganoid mythology, it is believed that the Mother of Gold's eternal light makes the plants in any biome grow faster, blessing the sea life within to be well-fed and overjoyed.

After a long swim, she finally reaches Mersinganoid Cove. The Mersinganoids gather around to greet her when she rises from the water and wraps each tentacle around a Violet Palm Tree nearby without ripping them off the ground. The Mersinganoids kneel and vibrate their fins on their cheeks as electrical pulses flash.

A cool thing about Mersinganoids is that their

hearts glow when they have very positive feelings, like love, friendship or joy. However, no matter the skin colour that they have, their blood is always red.

After kneeling to the Mother of Gold, the Mersinganoids would give her treasures that they stored for her, such as pearls and even the scales that came from their loved ones who had passed away.

I almost forgot to mention, like a protective mother, so that she never travels across the sea alone, she always brings her spawn with her, making sure they are always safe and with her.

Her young are unlike any other because her spawn is different from sea creatures. There was a prawn, a squid, an octopus, a crab, a sea angel–which is a very cute, transparent, fairy-like slug–a koi, a guppy, an eel, and finally, a goldfish that hadn't been born yet but had fully developed. They all shared her special light. But the youngest, being the little goldfish, was the most special. It was given a name: the Golden Starpearl. It shone like gold, was as bright as a star, and as small as a pearl. She would keep it in one of her tentacles, protecting it from anything that might try to steal it. But she knew she could trust the Mersinganoids. She showed the egg, and their sparkling eyes were all on it.

The closest Mersinganoid knelt down to the water, scooped it up with both their hands and reached for the Mother of Gold to drop the egg in. When she did, the Mersinganoid moved the egg closer to themselves, and a warm feeling filled them, making their hearts glow. The sound of their heartbeat made the egg glow a warm gold light as if the baby inside enjoyed it.

The other Mersinganoids did the same thing; they each scooped up water so they could take turns passing the egg around and feel that love soak into their veins. One by one, they each passed the egg around, feeling that love so much that some of them sighed joyfully, even hummed and offered compliments to it.

When the egg was eventually passed back to the same Mersinganoid, they gave it back to the Mother of Gold. Then they all sang to her.

The Mother of Gold really enjoyed listening to their mesmerising song, and she closed her one large eye and let their voices soothe her and her young.

They listened to their song until sunset and when the ocean darkened to an inky black. That signalled the Mother of Gold and her young to go home, back to the Deep Spirit Tree in the Twilight Zone.

That night, the clouds covered the sky, and a storm grew; the waves became violent and uncontrolled. Lightning struck the ocean's surface every minute. The young were close to the mother as she held them together in one giant tentacle, while in another was the tiny egg that was closer to the surface. The current was pulling them, but the Mother of Gold was strong enough to swim against it.

But as she did, lightning struck her tentacle that held the tiny egg, leaving the mother in pain. She opened it, and the strong current took away the egg. The mother realised her mistake and tried to grab it, but the current was so strong that it pulled the egg away from her, leaving her in fear. The egg was pulled further away from the family, eventually disappearing into the darkness of the depths.

The mother was devastated after losing the egg; she couldn't go after it because she worried that she would lose another one of her spawn in the storm. So, she had no choice but to keep going through the storm with her young, who had also seen everything that happened, leaving them devastated with her as they swam further and further away.

Months passed as the lost egg drifted through the biomes of the sea in the current, gradually entering shallower waters. It drifted into underwater meadows and forests, where saltwater Gippyguppies and other creatures noticed and watched as the egg drifted along with the current.

The egg was next taken to a mysterious biome where there were giant aquatic tree-like mushrooms whose roots stretched from the sand, and strange glowing sea slugs pollinated the dust the mushrooms produced.

Some noticed the egg and watched as it went along with the current, eventually disappearing.

The current gradually calmed down until the egg rolled onto the sand.

As time passed and summer approached, the egg rolled into shallow waters that were crystal clear, with coral everywhere, teeming with numerous reef creatures. The current finally disappeared, and the egg stopped in front of a rocky and sandy surface where a huge cave towered over it at the edge of a slope. The walls around the cave were covered in shellfish.

A few fish and eels found the egg and swam to investigate it, curious about where it came from. The eels circled it while the fish gently moved it around with their heads until a red tentacle suddenly shot out of the cave and towards them, scaring them so much that they fled.

Then two big and three small, glowing, beady yellow eyes appeared from the darkness, growling like a tiger. It hit its tentacle on the sand with frustration.

"Grr! They are so lucky," it grumbled, "I wish I could just have a bite of a school of fish. I'm starving."

The creature noticed the egg on the sand and picked it up before emerging out of the cave using another tentacle to rest its cheek against it.

The creature was a female Giant Spider Squid, an ambush predator that was meant to move into deeper waters to hunt but had decided to stay in the reef for longer. Her name was Pearl. She had six tentacles and five eyes, having lost one of her small eyes in a fight with her prey. She was as long and large as a palm tree.

She sighed heavily. "What do we have here? A fish egg that must've been moved out of its nest by accident. At least that's something to eat."

Her stomach–located above her head–growled in agreement. She opened her mouth, revealing her black, long and razor-sharp teeth with one that looked like the head of a spade drill, and tossed the egg inside, snapping it down in one gulp. Then she went back inside the cave to rest.

The inside of the cave had very few mossy and

decayed skeletons of fish that she had eaten when she was smaller. There was dead seagrass and bleached coral on the cave walls due to the lack of sunlight. Very few pearls were on the ground. She had collected them from clams and oysters around the reef and sometimes from logs that stretched out of the water, where small hooks hung down every now and then. Pearl's five yellow eyes provided the only light inside the cave. She swam to the middle of her lair to rest after consuming the egg.

An hour passed, and Pearl was fast asleep. The egg in her gut would have been digested by now. But because the egg came from the Mother of Gold, the outer layer resisted the corrosive enzymes trying to break it down.

The egg began glowing brighter until it could be seen from outside; the egg was ready to hatch!

The light awakened Pearl. "Where's that light coming from?" she asked herself, drowsily.

When she noticed the light inside her gut, she was shocked and immediately went off the ground, opened her mouth, and forced one of her tentacles in to grab the egg as quickly as she could. She pulled it out of her mouth and chucked the egg away from her. It floated in the water until it steadily sank to the ground, growing brighter and brighter as some dead plants on the stony ground turned green again, followed by sea moss and corals.

Pearl gasped when she saw everything change colour.

Then rays of light shot out of cracks around the

shell, and the egg burst into bits, revealing a bright light that had been born. Pearl covered her five eyes with her tentacles, even her lost one, as it was the most vulnerable.

As the light dimmed, she moved her tentacles off and saw a tiny, shiny goldfish lying on the ground, struggling to open its eyes.

Pearl's five eyes blinked twice in unison; then she rubbed them to check if it was real. It was real, and a tiny goldfish was in her lair!

She crept closer to the goldfish as it struggled to move and open its eyes and gently picked it up.

There were three orange crests shaped around the body like a triangle. Behind was a long and beautiful blue tail and two tiny fins under the goldfish's face. Smooth 'w' like patterns were between the body.

Pearl tilted her head to her right, then her left. The infant made high-pitched grunting sounds and finally adjusted its eyes for the first time. They were pink, and the pupils were white. It blinked until it saw Pearl.

"Such a shiny little baby you are," Pearl said to the fish.

"Hm?" The fish sounded like a baby girl.

"Your light revives the plants in my lair," Pearl answered as she looked around at the lively and luscious plants and corals. The little fish peeked over her large tentacle to see, then she turned back to her. "Mama?"

"No, I'm not your mother. I don't know where you came from, my shiny, fishy friend. But you look so precious. The world out there seems too dangerous.

Imagine how many predators, no matter the size, would be attracted to you if you attempted to set fin to the other side of the reef?"

"Pwedatos?" the fish asked, wondering what a predator was.

Pearl nodded. "I am an ambush predator here who is *very* hungry. It's hard to catch one when using very few things to lure them to me, and they know when I will strike." Her stomach growled, and her mind began to think the fish was food. "Just by thinking about it, you look kind of tasty for a small, easy, and golden vulnerable snack."

The newborn was so frightened that she burst into tears. Her tears, small yellow blobs of liquid gold drifted in the water, glowing brightly and slowly bouncing off the walls, making plants grow.

Pearl saw everything and was flabbergasted.

The fish calmed down and wiped her eyes, and the remaining golden tears floated away from her, lighting up the cave.

Pearl grabbed one blob to get a closer look at it. Then slowly, the blob began to solidify, turning into a golden pearl that sank down on her tentacle. Pearl thought, *What is she?*

She looked at the fish again, who stared at her in fear that she was about to swim away. But Pearl caught her and continued thinking as the fish struggled to escape. *If she is shiny and cries those weird teary blobs that turn into golden pearls, then where did she come from? How did she even get here?*

Her stomach growled again, stopping her from

thinking about how the tiny fish got here. Her mind began to slip into hunger that she growled at the fish. "Forget where you came from, little fish. I must satisfy my hunger!" She then slowly moved the tiny fish closer to her opened mouth.

The fish tried with all her might to escape her grasp. As she struggled, her light grew stronger until she flashed through the entire cave, blinding Pearl that she let go to rub all her eyes, allowing the fish to escape.

After furiously rubbing her eyes, Pearl lowered her tentacles and saw the fish swimming away as fast as she could.

"Hey! You get back here!" she yelled as she chased after her. Pearl tried to catch her with her six tentacles, but the fish managed to avoid all of them until she finally escaped to the light of the reef.

Pearl stopped at the mouth of the cave, furious at her failure that she hit the sand and growled at the fish as she swam away, finding somewhere to hide.

"You can swim, but you can't hide, little fish. I will find you!" she shouted before returning back into the darkness of her cave.

After swimming further into the unknown reef, the little fish eventually stopped to catch her breath. She then looked around her at new surroundings. Schools of fish were swimming everywhere, and eels waited in smaller tunnels for their next meals. All the fish were unfazed by her presence.

The little fish placed both of her tiny fins between her mouth and called, "Mama! Mama!"

But there was no answer.

She called again, "*Mama! Mama?*"

But there was no answer again.

Her fins dropped from her mouth as golden tears formed in her eyes and drifted into the surrounding waters, slowly turning into golden pearls as they sank to the sand.

She knew she was lost.

She blindly swam in the reef until she ran into a sandy gap, separating the reef from a nearby Kelp Forest. She entered the Kelp Forest, leaving a trail of shining golden tears behind her until she found small towers of mossy pebbles and shells stacked on top of each other. She swam there and laid herself in the middle of the stacks, covering herself with her blue tail. Her first horrible memories of Pearl flooded her mind:

The world out there seems too dangerous. Imagine how many predators, no matter the size, would be attracted to you? I am a predator who is very hungry. I will find you!

From those words Pearl said, the fish knew she wasn't safe. The only place where she would be safe was with her mother and nowhere else.

She covered her face with her long blue tail, closed her eyes and sobbed her tears that turned into golden pearls around her.

As night befell Hybrainia, the fish was buried in her golden pearls when a bright flash of light from the distance suddenly woke her up. She submerged out of her golden pearls and rose to the surface to investigate.

As half of her round body rose out of the water, she saw a bright light, bigger than the stars in the far ocean horizon. Her eyes slowly widened, and she softly grinned, immediately recognising that it was her mother.

She struggled to flashback but quickly realised that she would attract predators, even Pearl, if she tried. She also knew that she would be spotted in the darkness of the Kelp Forest. So, she went back down and hid in her golden pearls again to avoid attracting attention.

She needed to find a way to get home to her family, but how when she was so tiny and the world was way bigger than her?

She was vulnerable and helpless if she was ever to find a way home.

This is when the story begins

Chapter 1

A summer surprise for the Alphanians

The morning was beautiful in the Summertime, like how it was meant to be. Summer is the best season; it's the perfect time to swim, hang out with friends and have refreshing things to keep cool.

What's my favourite? Celebrations! On the twenty-fourth of December, we celebrate Christmas, and Pollen Village is lit up with colourful lanterns and decorations! Tar turns up the volume to max, and that makes the Singanoid villagers howl, scream happily and repeat. Some of the girls in my group would also perform, dancing and singing while the boys and I watched.

I don't like being on stage; I become anxious really easily.

When it's New Year's Eve, we make the firestar by creating our own shapes. Once they're done, I bring them together and shoot them up into the night sky, spreading joy around Hybrainia that a new year has been born!

But the Summertime had only just begun on day one.

Me and the team had grown a year older. I was finally sixteen. Bucky was eleven, Barbara was ten, Tar was my age, and so were Eric, Atom, Sandy and Stephenie. Violet was fifteen, and Chuckboi was seventeen, the eldest of my team.

I was sleeping in the Den, my head resting on Chuckboi's arm as if it were a pillow and his other arm over my body—his long red tail wrapped around me— keeping me warm and close. I snuggled as I was in a dream.

I was dreaming I was sitting by the dock of Pollen Village under a lilac sky. I was alone, but I didn't mind it at all as it was in my head. My Alphanian shoes were half under the water. I was watching the setting sun over the ocean horizon while the centre reflected the sun's light like a white shadow.

Then, from under the water's surface, I noticed a bright light, like a mini-star, rising from the darkness of the water, calling for me. It sounded quiet, but desperate as if the light needed my help. I leaned closer to the water and reached my hand for it. But as soon as my hand went under, it turned blue and split into three webbed fingers with spotty patterns on each one, lined up and all connected by a dark blue line that led down my hand.

That startled me and I quickly pulled my hand out of the water. I looked at my palm, and it was back to normal. I thought it was part of my dream.

The light called for me again. It came closer, closer and closer, and its call grew louder the nearer it was to me. I tried moving my hand down for it again, but was interrupted as I felt something pushing me, and my dream disappeared.

"Charlie! Chuck! Wake up! Wake up, sleepyheads! There's something that Violet and Eric want to show us!"

Chuckboi let go of me to stretch his arms and body. I stretched my arms, too, and they collapsed back on the pillows. Chuckboi did the same thing but with his arm over me again.

"C'mon, Charlie and Chuck! Get up, lazy nappers!"

"I don't wanna get up. Just ten more minutes," Chuckboi said tiredly.

I adjusted my eyes and saw Bucky with a very excited expression in his sparkling eyes and grin.

"W…what's up, buddy?" I asked with a yawn.

"Get up!" Bucky yelled continuously.

"Alright, alright! I'm getting up now." I moved Chuckboi's arm off me, and I sat up, rubbing my eyes.

We both looked at Chuckboi.

"C'mon, Chuck! Get up right now, you lazy Dragadillo!" Bucky said as he grabbed his tail and attempted to pull him. But he was too weak, and Chuckboi used his tail to wrap around Bucky's body and push him away.

Bucky got so annoyed at Chuckboi that he yelled, "*Wake up!*"

"Calm down, buddy. I know a way to wake him up," I said.

Bucky looked at me with surprise. "You do?"

I nodded. "It works all the time. Watch this. Chuckboi, if you get up, I'll give you a kiss."

Chuckboi immediately got up.

I burst out laughing as Bucky was startled when he

got up quickly.

"The power of the kiss raises the lazy Dragadillo."
I giggled.

"But you are gonna plant your sweet kiss on me,
right? On my cheek, I mean," Chuckboi asked, his face
turning pink, the same as his eyes.

I nodded and scooted closer to plant a kiss on his
cheek. I could hear his heart racing inside his chest.

"Thanks for the kiss, little Marshmallow," he said
with a sigh of adoration.

"You're welcome, Chuckboi. Also, Bucky wants to
show us something…or is it Violet and Eric who wants
to show us?" I asked Bucky.

"Eric and Violet want to show us something!"

"What is it?" Chuckboi asked.

"They said it was something fun, and they said that
you should bring your swimmers, Charlie."

"What for?" I asked him as I got to my feet. I went
down on my knees to match Bucky's size.

"Reasons!" he answered.

"Can't argue with that," I replied with a shrug. I went
back up and met Chuckboi's gaze as he got to his feet.
I smiled at him as he smiled back, lost in adoration, until
Bucky tapped my leg, getting my attention again. "You
guys coming or what?"

"Yes. I'll grab my swimmers in my art room."

"I'll wait for you, Charlie," Chuckboi insisted.

"Thank you."

"No problemo."

We walked out of the Den, and I went into my art
room to put on my swimmers. They hung by the right

side of my room, clean and shiny.

They were blue with a scaly pattern and sleeves that reached my elbows. The ends were yellow with an outline that passed from the sleeves, my armpits and to the bottom of the swimmers, circling around them. The top, where my head magically goes through, had a green lining on the inside, orange in the middle and yellow on the outside. A hole in the front allowed my amulet to show.

Atom made it for me for my sixteenth bloomday. I never used to have my own swimmers and just swam in my diamond armour. But thanks to Atom, I didn't need to do that anymore.

Once my swimmers were on, I went out of my art room, where Chuckboi and Bucky waited for the reveal. When they saw me, their eyes widened, and Chuckboi's face turned as pink as his eyes again.

"Wow! You look cool, Charlie!" Bucky giggled excitedly.

"Thanks, buddy. Chuckboi? What do you think?"

Chuckboi smiled, adoring my look. "Beautiful, little Marshmallow. You're like a water knight."

My cheeks went pink as I gripped my right arm and avoided his gaze for a second. "Thank you."

"C'mon! Let's get to the others in the shipyard!" Bucky said as he then ran to the stairs and up to the shipyard, where me and Chuckboi believed everyone else was waiting.

Chuckboi lent me his hand. I took it, and we went

up together.

I let him go out to the shipyard first, where everyone greeted him with smiles. I saw Violet wearing her black and blue shifting swimsuit that Atom also had made for her.

Most of my team members don't wear swimsuits; the only ones who do are Stephenie, Violet, and Tar, who only wear board shorts when swimming. It makes sense because Bucky, Sandy and Barbara are already aquatic beings. Reptiles like Eric, Chuckboi and Violet don't naturally wear swimsuits. However, having ADHD, Violet doesn't give a flip about what to wear and what not to wear.

When I got to the shipyard, and they saw me, their jaws dropped in amazement.

Atom placed his white hands on his cheeks, and tears of joy formed in his eyes. I immediately approached and wrapped my arms around him. "Oh, Atom. Don't cry. It's okay."

He wrapped his arms around me and trembled. "You're wearing the bloomday gift I made for you. I can't stop watching you grow." He began to cry loudly.

"Awww, Atom. That's very sweet. I love it; it's one of the best sixteenth bloomday gifts that I got from my team."

The girls thought it was very cute of Atom having his moment, and so did Chuckboi and Bucky. Eric thought it was pretty funny.

"Okay, Atom. Get a grip, and let's go to the surprise," Violet said, now a little impatient.

Eric nudged her shoulder. "Oh c'mon, babyface.

Let the molecule have his moment."

Eric and Violet have a relationship, just like me and Chuckboi and Stephenie, and Tar do.

Violet rolled her bright green eyes. "Fine."

When Atom finally calmed down and slipped his arms off me, he dried his eyes and took a deep breath. "I'm just so positively charged with joy for my best friend for life."

"Thank you, buddy," I said gratefully.

"Are you done yet, Mr Mollee?" Violet asked.

Atom's last name is Mollee.

He looked at her and nodded. "Yes, Violet. I'm done. I'm just very happy."

"Good. Now let's go to the thing that me and Eric want to show y'all. It's past Pollen Village! Tar and Stephenie are there, and they're having a—"

Just when she was about to spoil the surprise, Eric quickly placed his hand over her mouth. "No! Don't spoil it!"

"Oh...sorry, Eric," Violet's voice was muffled.

Eric moved his hand off her mouth.

"I'm always so bad at keeping things a surprise when I'm this excited," Violet confessed.

"It's okay, Violet; sometimes I'm in your shoes, too," I replied.

She looked at me with confusion. "But I don't wear shoes!"

"It's an expression. It means to empathise with someone else...I think," Chuckboi answered.

Violet now understood.

Then Sandy, who was a little impatient with the

moments we were having, sighed and asked all of us, "Why are we still here? Violet? Eric? Are you going to show us the 'surprise'?"

"Oh, yes! Let's get to the surprise! Follow us!" Violet said as she went for the ladder on the left side of the ship. In the blink of an eye, Eric beat her to the green grass without her knowing until she saw him.

He snickered at her and said, "Slowpoke."

"Show off!" Violet yelled.

Eric likes to beat anyone in a race, but he always gets too excited every time he wins and calls people slow pokes, which is not very funny to them. When it comes to Eric's racing games, there are no rules; the only rule that he always says is to beat the opponent, and he takes that too seriously.

As our other friends went down the ladder one at a time, Chuckboi and I walked to the ledge when Eric shouted at us, "C'mon, slowpokes! We don't have all day!"

Upon hearing that, Chuckboi stared directly into his blue eyes with a look of annoyance. "Eric, we do have all day! I don't wanna start this again!"

Eric laughed at him as he hyped himself up. "Well, I do! I wanna race you to the surprise! You're just saying that because you're jealous of my speed!"

Chuckboi's eyes narrowed. "I'm really not."

"Well, it may seem that you aren't; I know deep down inside that pumpin' muscle of yours you are just being chicken. C'mon! I wanna race!" Eric yelled back, determined.

Chuckboi growled and rolled his eyes. "Fine!" He

then tried to climb over the ledge of the ship, but I nabbed his tail to stop him. He looked at me as I shouted to Eric, "Not today, Eric. You and Violet want to show us a surprise. We don't want to turn it into absolute chaos because you want to race. We'll race next time, okay?"

Eric stopped hyping himself, and a look of disappointment crept into his face, and his body turned pale green. "Aw, man."

Chuckboi smiled at me. "Thanks, little Marshmallow."

I nodded in response. Then I gestured with my head to insist he go down first, but he shook his head and replied, "Marshmallows first."

I cackled at his clever answer, then climbed over the ledge and jumped to the dock below, ignoring the ladder. Chuckboi finally joined me and the group, and Violet and Eric began leading us to the surprise.

We made our way through the forest and eventually to Pollen Village, where no Singanoid was strangely seen.

Most of us were confused until Violet told us they were at the surprise that was held in the Oceanic Mountainside, which was past the dock and further up the beach. We continued through the village until we reached the dock, where we saw the mountains that stretched from the water.

We call it the Oceanic Mountainside because of the huge mountains that protrude from the water. Through a small entrance, inside are shallow rock lagoons where the Singanoids sometimes go to relax, collect pearls to sell, and sometimes look for smaller animals that live inside smaller pools for fun; it's the Singalings who do that often. Sometimes, I go there to help the villagers look for pearls. I do get sidetracked if something catches my attention, and I go and inspect whatever it is. But I do go back on track when they call my name.

As we got closer to the Oceanic Mountainside, we started hearing music blasting from the lagoons, and we saw someone who was wearing a black and lavender-shifting tight swimsuit with a large orangey-yellow flower pattern on her left side, almost wrapping around to her right. Her hand was on a palm tree, releasing neon green magic into the tree's vascular system.

When she noticed us, it turned out to be Stephenie. She waved at us as we approached her.

"Stephenie!" I exclaimed, "You're in your swimsuit too!"

She giggled. "I am. You're in yours that Genshi made for you!"

"I am! It's been a while since I've seen you use your magic!"

"This tree needed care. So, I did what was right for nature," Stephenie explained.

Believe it or not, Stephenie isn't just called the Green Nature for nothing; not only can she play the flute and violin, but she also has the powers to heal plants and help them bloom. Amazingly, she can sense their needs and uses her magic to give them what they require. She loves to meditate in the wilderness and watch it flourish peacefully. Sometimes, she would watch the ocean from afar, even the waves as they splash onto the sand majestically.

I smiled widely at her. "That's very sweet of you to do that."

Everyone agreed.

Finally, Violet said to all of us as she started hopping and beaming in great excitement, "I bet Tar is waiting for us. He's the one who made the surprise! Let's get into the lagoons and be surprised!"

Eric agreed with her, and he turned a bright yellow. "Let's go!"

Then Violet and Eric dashed through the entrance as we followed behind. When we entered the lagoons, our jaws dropped in amazement!

All of the Singanoid villagers were there, having the time of their lives, jumping off the tall beach cliffs and splashing into the largest lagoon that was at the back of the mountains with a view of the ocean! Some other Singanoids chilled in the shallower lagoons, having a refreshing drink of Sapphire Melon juice from clay cups from the village.

We saw Tar and Violet on a large rock on the left-hand side of the lagoons, playing upbeat party music from his small but loud DJ booth as Violet sang. A few of the Singanoids danced to the music, whooping and howling at the same time!

When Tar saw us, he waved, smiled widely and shouted, "So glad you made it, dudes! Surprise! Join the fun and go crazy!"

We waved back and smiled widely at him.

"*This is awesome!*" Sandy squealed excitedly.

"*I can't wait to have fun!*" Barbara added. Sandy and Barbara immediately went to the largest lagoon, and Bucky followed them. Stephenie went to Tar to boogie with the music.

Me, Chuckboi and Atom looked at each other and started laughing excitedly.

"Violet's truly right! Let's have the best first day of the Summertime *ever!*" Atom said.

We both agreed and then I wondered, "Where should we start first?"

"Why not start with a swim in the lagoon?" Chuckboi suggested.

We agreed with that idea and then headed to one of the lagoons that was empty of people to start having fun. Atom went in the water first, diving down with a gentle splash. Chuckboi went in next, feet first.

Finally, it was my turn. I took off my green and blue Alphanian shoes and placed them beside me before moving my feet into the beautiful water. But after submerging my feet completely, I started feeling a strong tingle that made me quickly pull them out and let out a yelp. Chuckboi and Atom saw my reaction.

"Are you okay? What's wrong?" Chuckboi asked worriedly.

"What happened?" Atom asked, suddenly confused.

I shrugged. Then I started noticing my feet slowly turning dark blue, and they changed into webbed flippers!

Our eyes widened in disbelief.

"What just freaking happened to my feet?" I exclaimed.

Atom approached closer and leaned over without bending his green legs—because he couldn't—and inspected to process what had happened. After a moment, his eyes glanced at me, and a wide, amazed grin filled his face. "It's about to happen!"

"What's about to happen? Why do my feet look like this?" I asked.

"I remember discovering Mindoglyphics about this back when I was a kid! It is believed that the Mindatar unlocks her powers from the water shrine, and her water powers develop! That was late...probably because you weren't in the water often or that it required time to *fully* develop," Atom wondered. "Why don't we go somewhere private to activate them?"

If you may be wondering what Mindoglyphics are or what they mean, they are the ancient arts of Hybrainia from a long time ago, even before I bloomed. They were meant to tell stories of their beliefs and of me, their goddess.

Chuckboi and I looked at each other for a moment to think, then back at Atom.

"Where are you thinking?" I asked.

"I know a place around here. Follow me!"

He then went out of the water. Chuckboi got out second, but I was last as I was struggling to get up. Chuckboi picked me up, and we followed Atom as we made our way through the lagoons, all the way to a narrow gap, which Atom had to squeeze through. By the time me and Chuckboi got to the gap, my feet slowly turned back to normal, thanks to the sun.

We watched as Atom made it to the other side. "It's just right here!" he shouted.

Chuckboi put me down, and I shrunk down to Bucky's size and ran to the other side as he squeezed his way to us.

When I made it to the other side of the gap, I realised I had entered a secret cenote.

The sky was mostly hidden by the mountain's rock, and a hole above the water allowed sunlight to reflect on the cave ceiling. The water was so clear that we could see stalactites full of corals glowing a handful of hues in the darkness.

I grew back to my normal size and walked closer to the water as my curiosity grew.

Chuckboi finally caught up to us, and his eyes grew wide at seeing the cenote.

"How long has this cenote been here?" I asked Atom.

"I sometimes come here to extract things to study back in my lab."

"How do you study from under the water?" Chuckboi asked.

"With a drone, of course. I made it look like me. I made it copy my movements and speech," Atom explained.

"Yo! That's impressive. Your intelligence has been at a whole new level since we first met! When are you gonna start teaching students?"

He smirked, knowing I was joking. "I'd rather tell than teach."

"Fair enough, dude."

I faced the water again. Then Atom finally said, "Jump in. I wanna see your abilities shine."

"Is it safe?" I asked.

"As far as I know, yes," he answered sincerely.

I sighed with relief. "Alright. On three, I will jump in. One…two…"

"*Three!*" A voice suddenly shouted, and I was forcefully pushed into the cenote, splashing into the water.

I held my breath as I stopped a couple of metres down from the surface. I looked up and saw Chuckboi and Atom yelling at a green figure that looked like Eric. I growled, and bubbles escaped my mouth. But then, suddenly, I began to feel like my breath was taken from me, and I sank deeper from the surface.

I struggled to swim to the surface while waving my arms crazily to get my friends' attention. But as I did, my head started to feel light, and I stopped waving my arms and kicking my feet. My vision blurred, and I saw the surface rising further away from me. My vision faded away, and the sounds around me grew quieter.

It was like I was sleeping without being allowed to breathe.

A few seconds had passed, and I began to see a faint golden light growing under my closed eyelids and a distorted black figure appeared in front of me. It whispered to me, saying to wake up and that it needed my help. The figure then transformed into a round fish with three tips around its head, and the light grew brighter, as if it was showing me something.

Suddenly, the light disappeared, and I regained consciousness. My eyes opened, and I gasped heavily as if there were air. Then, a burst of energy escaped from my body and into the surrounding waters, even to the surface, where it released a huge splash.

I steadied my breathing and realised I was lying at the bottom of the underwater cave. I got up and looked around as a mix of emotions filled my body.

How am I breathing? I couldn't do that before. What was also that voice and those visions?

Not knowing, I scratched my head and immediately noticed my hand was different. I looked at it and saw it had split into three webbed fingers, exactly the same as the one from my dream! I twisted and turned my body with amazement.

Then, as I did, I caught a glimpse of something hiding behind rocks full of glowing corals and stalagmites further in the dark cave; two small, glowing teal cat eyes were watching me.

It knew it had been spotted because it emerged from its hiding place and swam directly to me. From what was partially revealed by the vibrant-coloured lights of the corals, its body was scaly and looked very similar to a Singanoid. Its flippers and fins around its face glowed sky blue.

I heard it whisper, but I didn't know what it said.

I never took my eyes off it.

By the time it was about to emerge from the darkness, I heard a splash from above me, startling the figure and causing it to vanish back into the darkness.

"No, wait! Come back!" I shouted to the creature.

But it was gone.

I looked up and saw Eric, who must've been pushed or thrown into the water because of how intense the splash was. I swam up to him. But at that moment, maybe by how I moved my hand, Eric was pulled directly to me within seconds and I was startled. "Sorry Eric! Are you good?"

He looked at me, and his face expressed as if he was trying to say, 'Do *I look like I'm good?*'. But it quickly changed by seeing my appearance and his body turned yellow.

That means he's amazed, hyper, or really, really excited.

I chuckled. "I know! I look different, don't I?"

He nodded as he placed one hand over his mouth and pointed to the surface.

I understood and said, "Let me try something." I raised my hand slowly from in front of Eric to the surface, and he rose back up at exactly the same speed as my hand until half his body protruding out.

I laughed, amazed that it worked.

Finally, I swam to the surface once Eric had been pulled out.

As my head rose out of the water, Atom's jaw dropped, and Chuckboi's eyes grew wide.

"Ta-da! Surprise!" I said.

"It worked! It actually worked! You discovered your first form!" Atom hopped around and started laughing joyfully.

I wanted to try something else and see if the water could bring me to the ground.

So, I moved both my hands up, and the water around me rose higher. It brought me straight to my friends before splashing onto the ground.

"Okay, that was cool!" I said.

"I agree, little Marshmallow," Chuckboi replied, "How did you do that?"

"Magic!" I raised my hands up and the water below me floated in the air around us. When I dropped my hands, so did the droplets.

"Okay, now that's cool," I said, "I wonder what other abilities I have?"

"Why don't you test them here?" Chuckboi suggested.

"Anywhere but here is fine; this place isn't safe," a female voice said from the gap.

We all looked and saw a familiar figure emerging from it.

It turned out to be Kira because we saw her placing her golden prosthetic arm onto the rock to squeeze herself through.

Kira is the chief of Pollen Village because she wears a necklace with a special crystal. Honestly, I had no idea how long she's had it, but she must've had it even before her battle scars. She was turquoise with purple eyes. Half of her hair was black, with one violet-tipped braid resting over her left shoulder, while the other was shaved off and patterned with swirls and stripes, showing a huge horizontal blue scar that almost touched her eyebrow. She wore a white singlet that had blue shoulder straps and a brown leather skirt with a black belt keeping it up. Her gold prosthetic arm on her left also had swirls but no fingers.

Kira is very positive and understands the whole village and us Alphanians. Sometimes, she's very strict when it comes to following her rules to keep her people and us safe.

"I was worried someone would find the cenote," she said softly. She saw me and smiled. "You discovered your first form! I'm proud o' you, sweetheart. However, you should've done it somewhere else, not here."

I tilted my head. "Why not, Kira?"

"This cenote was where I lost my arm, and I took out one of its eyes," she answered.

Shock punched us in our guts because we remembered she first told us about an incident that she had a couple of years ago.

"Oh! Right! You told us how you lost your arm…from, like a…squid, wasn't it?" Eric stuttered, his body shifting to a pale white.

"A Giant Spider Squid," Kira answered.

Atom freaked out when Kira said 'spider'. "Spider? Where?"

"She said 'Spider Squid', you dork," Chuckboi said.

"Oh, that's a relief."

Slowly, my shock faded away, and I started wondering why it was called a Giant Spider Squid. I tried to imagine it in my head, but for some reason, it felt impossible as my thoughts didn't feel like my own, and I wasn't sure why.

Finally, Kira spoke again. "I apologise for not telling you about this place, but I thought it was best not to tell anyone about it. Since I overheard Atom saying that he's been here a few times, I'll let it slide for once. But if I catch you going in or out of the cenote again, you'll be grounded for a day. Do I make myself clear?"

We nodded.

"Crystal, Kira," I replied.

"Good. Now get your butts out of here."

Eric, Atom, and Chuckboi headed to the gap first and squeezed through to rejoin the party. I was last to go through because I struggled to walk as I was still in my water form. Also, something inside of me made me feel drawn to the cenote, so I stopped in front of the gap and stared at the water. My mind began to feel uneasy, the sounds around me got quieter and the same voice whispered to me again, saying to enter the cenote and find 'her'.

But I was snapped back to reality when Kira approached and gently smacked my face.

"Sorry I kept you waiting. I must've dozed off. I'll squeeze through now," I said as I made my way through the gap, and she followed me back to the others.

After getting back to everyone else in the lagoons, Chuckboi and Atom were there, but Eric had wandered off to relax or to hang out with Violet.

They turned to me and greeted me with gentle smiles.

"Took you a bit," Atom said.

"I didn't take that long, did I?" I asked, worried.

Chuckboi shook his head. "He's just joking."

I carefully moved further from the gap to let Kira

through. When I went under the sunlight, the water I was carrying dried up, and I noticed myself slowly turning back to normal. I looked at my hands as they turned back to white and my fingers merged.

"So good to be back to normal," I said.

"Interesting. So when you're under the sun, you turn back to normal after some time," Atom murmured after observing what happened.

"Why don't you three relax by the lagoons and keep having some fun?" Kira suggested.

We agreed.

Then we heard Stephenie calling to us. We turned and saw her by the same lagoon where I had left my shoes, waving at us. We immediately came to her and she gave me my shoes. But I told her to leave them on the ground as we were gonna go back in, and she understood.

"You're not gonna believe what Charlie has discovered!" Atom exclaimed.

Stephenie tilted her head. "What did you discover, Char'i?"

I stepped into the water, and my foot changed back into my flipper.

Her eyes widened as she covered her mouth. "You discovered your aquatic form! I'm so proud of you!"

I chuckled as I sat down in the water, submerging my legs completely as they turned into webbed feet, and bioluminescent patterns reappeared.

Atom and Chuckboi joined me, and we all relaxed and chatted for some time.

When time flew by until the sky began to turn

purple, everyone was exhausted after having a fun day in the lagoons in the Oceanic Mountainside, as we were.

Tar packed up his booth and carefully made his way down the rocks and everyone made their way out of the lagoons, through the beach and back to Pollen Village.

I held Bucky like a baby as he had fallen asleep in my arms while Barbara slept in Stephenie's.

Making our way back through Pollen Village and the forest that separated our ship from them, I looked at the sky and remembered that it was also from my dream. I closed my eyes and smiled.

When we finally reached the Alphanian Ship, one by one, my friends climbed up the ladder until it was me, Bucky, and Chuckboi who climbed last. Chuckboi kindly took Bucky out of my arms with his tail and insisted I go first. So, I did, as he climbed up the ladder below me.

When we were in the shipyard, Chuckboi gave me Bucky back, and we made our way down the stairs, through the hallway and finally to the Den. I gently laid Bucky down on the soft pillows to sleep. To keep him warm, I grabbed a blanket from under the pillows that I sometimes use in case I got cold and laid it over him. That made him smile, grab the blanket and pull it over half of his head. I chuckled softly, happy that he was warm and comfortable as he drifted into a deep sleep.

I then walked to my art room to change into my jammies before returning back to the Den with Bucky. I lay down next to him, wrapped my arm over him and closed my eyes to go to sleep.

My Alphanians were close to going to sleep too as they were very tired from today. Moment after moment, I heard their footsteps enter the Den, and their soft breaths as they fell asleep.

Eventually, I felt an arm wrapping over me and pulling me close as a gentle kiss was planted on the back of my head. I smiled as I knew that it was Chuckboi.

After a bit of time, I drifted into a deep sleep.

Chapter 2

A mysterious voice

I slept soundly through most of the night. When it felt like it was past midnight, I was having a dream.

But this was no ordinary dream; I started seeing the light again, but this time it was brighter. The same figure that was round with three tips around its body appeared in the centre of the light, and I heard the same whispers: '*Enter the water! Please find her! Bring her back to me! I've lost her and I need your help!*'

The whispers of distress raced around my head all at once and disrupted what was once my peaceful slumber. The whispers made it harder and harder to stay asleep until my head started to hurt, and I finally woke up.

I found myself still in the Den. Chuckboi's arm was off me, and I was facing him. I must've tossed and turned while having that abstract dream. I sighed with relief that I hadn't woken him up.

Then a second later, the thought of the cenote in the Oceanic Mountainside clouded into my head, and the whispers came back, telling me to go there.

I grasped my head tightly and furiously closed my eyes as I started getting sick of hearing the voice telling me to go to the cenote that Kira said not to go.

Whatever you are, you're gonna get me in trouble if I go there, I thought.

But the voice continued begging until I had no choice but to do it. *Alright! Alright! Fine! But if I get caught by Kira, I'll blame you for this!*

Slowly and quietly, I got to my feet and snuck out of the Den to get to my art room.

It was very dark, so I tread carefully as my eyes glowed blue. Once I reached my art room, I took off my jammies to put on my swimmers as quietly as I could, then gradually made my way through the dark corridor, up the stairs and finally to the shipyard.

Millions of stars twinkled in the night sky, and the Silver Moon was in its waning crescent.

I walked to the left side of the ship, hopped over the ledge and climbed down the ladder to the dock below.

Once my feet touched the wood, I started running, making my way through the forest until I reached the sight of Pollen Village on the other side. I crept through the sleeping village until I reached the beach, where I ran until finally getting to the Oceanic Mountainside. I entered inside, where I saw most of the rock lagoons while the rest hid in the shadows.

I had never realised how dark this place gets at night. I need to remember where the gap that Atom showed me and Chuckboi is. I hope my glowing eyes can reveal it.

I walked close to the walls and used my glowing eyes to find the gap, even using my hands to feel it from the darkness. It took a bit of time before I finally found it.

I carefully squeezed through until I reached the other side, where I saw the glowing colourful lights deeper in the cenote's forever calm water.

I walked to the edge to see the corals below as a nervous feeling began to fill my stomach. I really didn't want to do it as I knew I would get in trouble, but I had to for whatever that mysterious voice was telling me.

I looked up to my forehead and said softly, "You better be serious with me jumping in, mysterious voice."

The voice said that it was truly being honest and really needed my help.

I was a bit suspicious, but the voice did sound sincere because of its desperate tone.

I took one more step forward and was about to jump into the water.

Suddenly, I heard a noise from inside the gap.

I sharply turned as I began to sweat in fear, worried that Kira was coming.

But when they emerged from the gap, it turned out to be just Atom and Chuckboi.

"Atom? Chuckboi?" I exclaimed quietly, confused and full of dismay.

"Charlie?" Atom replied.

"What are you two doing here?" I asked.

"We should be asking the same of you," he replied.

"And I should be asking back!"

We paused for a moment.

Finally, Chuckboi spoke. "We noticed you were up to something. We followed you all the way here!"

"But why?" I asked.

"We're concerned about you. Having known you since childhood, we know you wouldn't randomly act like this," Atom answered.

"Exactly!" I exclaimed. Then I took a deep breath to calm down, and said, "Boys, listen to me; I'm very obedient with rules. But something is telling me to come here to find 'her' by entering into the cenote. Call me crazy, because I might be."

Atom and Chuckboi looked at each other, trying to process what I told them. Then they turned back to me.

"A voice?" Atom asked, "Since when did you start hearing a voice?"

"When I was pushed into the cenote, which I know was done by Eric."

"I threw him in the water too, to teach him a lesson," Chuckboi added.

"This was what I heard from the voice: '*wake up. I need your help! Please find her. I lost her and I need your help*'. I even had visions as to what it was trying to tell me. I doubt it was just a dream."

Atom pondered for another moment, then looked at the wall to notice some coal. He walked to the wall and attempted to carefully tear some off with his bare white hands, but had no luck.

"What are you doing, Atom?" Chuckboi asked, confused.

"Chucky? Can you tear some of this rock off here?"

He walked to the small coal vein, grabbed a chunk and used his strength to tear it off the wall to give to Atom. Atom retrieved it and walked straight to me, handing the coal to me. "Draw what you saw with this."

I took the coal and used my powerful strength in both my hands to break it in half, and started drawing on the flat ground what the visions were. Then I got up and stood back for Atom and Chuckboi to take a closer look.

After examining the pictures, Atom looked at me with a curious frown, and his eyebrows raised. "Are they what you saw?"

I nodded.

Then suddenly, out of nowhere, a flash of light burst from under the water, and our heads immediately turned to the water as the light quickly faded.

Stunned with astonishment, the light seemed familiar to the one from my visions that the voice was showing me.

"Woah! What was that?" Chuckboi exclaimed.

Atom stuttered as his mind was unable to process what had just happened. Eventually, his words came back, and he exclaimed, "*I had never seen that before!*"

Chuckboi quickly covered Atom's mouth because of how loud and shocked he was. "Atom! Keep it down! We don't wanna get caught!"

While he shushed Atom, my eyes never left the water as the sounds around me faded. I heard the voice in my head again in distress. *Follow her! Find her! Please! Bring her back to me! I'm worried about her!*

Slowly, I took small steps closer to the water. I got closer and closer to the water until I was about to jump in. But I was caught in Chuckboi's arms and tail. The sounds returned, and I heard his voice from behind. I shook my head as he turned to face me by moving his flexible tail. "What are you doing? You were about to jump in the water!"

I glanced at the water behind me.

"Yes, that water," Chuckboi replied.

The voice in my head continuously begged for me to jump in as I remembered the bright flash of golden light that had happened seconds ago. Finally, I turned my head back to him and said, "Drop me in."

His face changed to a very shocked expression at what he had just heard. "Why?"

"The voice is begging me to go in. Whatever that light was, the voice desperately wants me to find it," I answered.

Chuckboi paused to think. But Atom agreed with me. "Good thing I brought my drone, boy," he said as he rushed to the gap and came back with his drone. He put it on the ground in front of him.

"Why do you have your drone?" I asked.

Chuckboi's eyes narrowed. "I asked him the exact same thing when we got here."

"I mean…it wouldn't hurt to gain a bit more research. Plus, I recommend having someone with you when exploring something like this," he answered.

"Touche," I said. "Okay, once me and Atom find the source of that light the voice is telling me to find, we'll return to the surface before sunrise and tell Kira about this. But we cannot let her find out we have been in here again."

"But what if she comes?" Chuckboi asked,

concerned.

"If you both hear footsteps, find somewhere to hide and warn me not to return back here," suggested.

Atom and Chuckboi looked at each other for a moment. Atom agreed as he must've thought it was the best idea, so Chuckboi agreed, too.

Finally, his eyes met mine again. "Just…be careful, okay? Remember Kira mentioned how she lost her arm to a predator in this cenote?"

I nodded. "I'll keep my eyes peeled."

Chuckboi let out a deep sigh.

"I'll be right behind you, Charlie; I just need to set this mode in my goggles to pair with my drone," Atom said as he moved his goggles over his eyes and moved his hands around. From his eyes, there were multiple screens around him. We just saw him move his hands around in the air.

As Atom began to take control of the drone on the ground, it started mimicking his movements and oral speech. He was as ready as I was to search for the mysterious light.

Chuckboi took a few steps away from the water before putting me down, and he moved his hand under my cheek.

I placed my hand over his and closed my eyes. When I opened them back up, I said to Chuckboi, "I'll be back as soon as I can before sunrise. If you two hear footsteps approaching, run and hide."

He and Atom nodded again.

Finally, I turned to the water and slowly made my way in. My feet turned into flippers as the rest of my body submerged into the calm water, changing into my aquatic form until I was completely under.

Atom's drone splashed in behind me and grasped onto my back as we began making our way into the underwater cave.

It was really dark, as the only lights were the glowing corals beneath us and the bioluminescence on my legs, flippers, arms and eyes.

As we went further in, the number of corals slowly decreased. Atom transformed one of his drone arms into a flashlight, making navigating through the cave much easier. He moved the light around and revealed something unusual on the cave walls; there were pictures of the creature that looked like a Singanoid I had seen before. Others had a weird-looking squid with six tentacles and a long, wavy fin on the back.

Atom's curiosity grew towards the pictures he got of me and approached to take a closer look. I followed him as he began taking pictures to study later.

"These pictures are interesting! They show two specimens of what looks to be a Singanoid with flippers and cheek fins and a squid," Atom mumbled.

"I definitely saw something watching me when I was pushed into the cenote yesterday; it looks very similar to that one," I pointed at the picture of the Singanoid-looking creature. "Most of all, there's no picture of that 'Giant Spider Squid' Kira told us about."

"True. Whatever that thing is, I hope it doesn't have spider features."

"Hence its name, Atom. What else would it be? Perhaps it acts like an ambush predator of some sort."

He gripped back onto me, and we continued our way through the cave with his flashlight, even using the small, weak groups of corals as our guide.

Keep going! She's around here somewhere! I heard the voice say in my mind.

We're working on it!

Making our way further into the cave, we had to swim over stalagmites, under stalactites and even through some small spaces until we saw rays of moonlight on the sand at the very end of the cave. Shadows over the moon rays looked like there was a Kelp Forest nearby.

There was no sign of the gold light in the cave, as we thought it must've escaped into the Kelp Forest. So we swam out of the cave and kept looking in the biome.

Atom shut off his flashlight arm to avoid attracting the attention of bigger predators that could be anywhere.

We searched high and low and left and right, even moving rocks and fallen kelp to search. We avoided sleeping creatures like sharks and stingrays on the seabed, as I thought it was breathtaking to see. Eventually we found a flat rock covered in sea moss with small stacks of pebbles on top and a pile of golden pearls in the middle.

Another point of interest! I thought.

We approached as Atom took pictures. I carefully grabbed a few golden pearls without knocking over any of the stacks and wondered if they were actually made of gold because they were clean and shiny, and I could even see my own distorted reflection in them. So I asked Atom to have a look at them and he took one from me to scan it.

After a moment of studying the pearl, his eyes widened, his eyebrows raised and his jaw dropped.

"What is it made of?" I asked, puzzled.

He glanced at me and replied, "It's pure *Au!*"

A mix of amazement and bewilderment filled me when I heard that. "Pure gold? How are there pearls made of pure gold?"

"I…can't explain. Pearls are only made by oysters. This is impossible!"

"Why don't we hold one to take back to study and keep searching for that light?"

Atom nodded and pressed a small button on his blue metal chest and it opened a cavity within. He tossed the pearl inside before closing it back up. He then went onto my back again and we continued searching.

We went over small stone hills and followed the seabed as it dropped down until it stopped at a towering wall of kelp, where the top aquatic leaves almost touched the water's surface.

"We've searched literally everywhere! No sign of the light in the cave and Kelp Forest," Atom said, feeling a bit hopeless.

"What about beyond here? The light could have escaped through the kelp," I wondered.

Atom looked concerned. "I'm not sure. We're already past ten metres from the surface. The deeper we go, the more unknown and dangerous the chances are we'll be hunted."

"But we can't give up now! The voice really wants me to find that light."

"Sunrise is only an hour away."

"That's still enough time to search for the light. C'mon, we have to do this, we are Alphanians, and we are in this together," I said as I held Atom's drone cheeks.

Atom paused to think about it. Eventually, he answered, "You're right, Alpha. We mustn't back out."

"That's the spirit, dude! I'll go first." I was about to move the long kelp out of the way, but Atom stopped me and insisted he would go first.

"Are you sure?"

He nodded. "Charged with positivity in my nucleus! Plus, I could make another one of these if necessary. I have the blueprint and materials."

"Alright, fair enough," I replied.

"I will make sure it's safe." He slipped through the kelp and a huge gasp was heard from him. "You need to see this!" he exclaimed.

I took a deep breath and swam through.

When I saw the other side, my breath was taken away and my eyes widened.

Thousands of different vibrant colours lit up the darkness of the water. Large limestone rocks and small mountains were everywhere, teeming with corals, plants and hundreds of species of fish. Sand blanketed the seafloor and some of the rocks.

We had just stumbled into a huge, healthy

communal coral reef!

"This…is…unreal!" I exclaimed.

"There's so much data here!" Atom's eyes were dilated, and he laughed in excitement.

"It looks like a place you could easily get lost in," I said.

"No joke, Charlie!"

Finally, I refocused on the task the voice had given me, and said to Atom, "C'mon. Let's find that gold light."

He agreed, and we both swam into the reef.

Chapter 3

A world of colour and life

This new world was fascinating and beautiful. A lot of fish swam past us while some others approached me, like a school of orange and white striped angelfish with sharp vertical fins that looked like crescents of the Silver Moon. They surrounded me as they showed a happy expression on their side-faced eyes. It made me laugh until I heard an unfamiliar voice coming from one of them! "She's finally arrived!"

I turned to the fish that spoke and said in an astonished tone, "Did you just talk?"

The fish nodded. "Yes, Mindatar! We did!"

I paused as no words could describe how flabbergasted I was. I turned to Atom. "Are you hearing this?"

But Atom gave me a confused expression. "Hear… what?"

In your aquatic form, you have the ability to understand what any sea creature says, the voice told me.

I understood and told Atom. "It turns out when I'm in my aquatic form, I have the ability to understand what any sea creature says."

Hearing that, Atom beamed and started laughing. "*That's…!*" he shouted, but then his voice was muffled for a second. Finally, he said in a quieter tone, almost like an exclaimed whisper, "That's incredible! So you can understand what any sea creature says?"

"That was exactly what I said; the voice in my head told me just then," I answered.

"Understandable," Atom replied. He then suggested that I ask the fish around us if they saw the light.

I thought that was a good idea, so I did just that and asked if they saw any golden light pass by.

The fish looked at each other and pondered, mumbling to one another, until they all looked at me again. "No. But we saw golden pearls scattered in trails all over the reef. Maybe they can lead you to that light, but be careful as our apex predator is also around."

One of them swam closer to me and whispered, "She shares the name of those round objects on the grains of sand seen all over the reef."

"So her name is Pearl?" I asked.

The fish nodded.

I smiled and nodded back. "We'll keep a lookout."

"Stay safe and find what you are looking for!" they replied.

I told everything to Atom so he understood what they said, and then we made a move on, looking for more golden pearls scattered in trails. It didn't take much time until we found a trail; their glimmer reflected the Silver Moon's light.

We followed the trail through the reef as we also

kept a look out for 'Pearl' and the light.

The further we went into the reef, the more interesting things we found along the way. Atom took pictures of corals, fish and plants to study later.

Eventually, the trail of golden pearls led us to a massive sandy concave slope, where there were rocks, shellfish and plate corals everywhere, when I caught a shiny glimpse of a pile of golden pearls at the entrance of a dark cave further down. Other trails from different areas of the reef all ended in the pile of pearls. We swam to the pile of pearls.

"The pearls end here, but still no sign of the light," Atom said.

"All the other trails scattered from all over the reef lead to this one spot. Don't you find that uncomfortably suspicious?" I asked.

He looked at me with his eyes full of concern. "Some predators do this to lure their prey. I've seen it in the wild before."

That seemed to confirm my suspicion that we must've been lured. It all explained why the trails all led to this dark cave. "Then we should leave immediately as this could be a trap."

Atom agreed. So we both swam back up, but then Atom must've seen something below me so he screamed, "*Look out!*"

But I was too slow to react; then something grabbed my foot and pulled me into the darkness of the cave in less than two seconds!

Whatever was holding me took me deeper in at a very quick speed until I must've reached its lair or den because I was thrown onto something soft and slimy. I rapidly looked around in fear and confusion as to what was going on.

Then five glowing yellow eyes appeared right in front of me, staring with a terrifying growl. More fear struck my chest, and I tried to back away.

But the eyes moved closer. As they did, small blobs of light escaped from what looked like seagrass and slowly lit up part of the cave, revealing tentacles moving over the seagrass.

Then it shot one of its tentacles at me. I reacted quickly that time and tried to whack it away with my eyes tightly closed. But after I did, the creature screamed in pain and something lay on me. I opened my eyes to see what had just happened and saw the tentacle was cut off and lying on my body. I quickly pushed it away and gagged, "Ew! Ew! That is disgusting!"

The tentacle lay motionless on the seagrass. I looked at my hand and saw it had turned into a sharp, webbed and bladed weapon!

"So that's how!" I said, stunned.

Suddenly, a light appeared from above a hole, and the drone of Atom appeared. He saw me and shouted, "There you are! Hurry, and let's get you out of here!"

I wasted no time and immediately swam up for Atom, but my foot was caught again by the creature's tentacle.

Atom turned off his light before he was seen as he trembled in fear.

I attempted to shake off the tentacle, but the

creature refused to let me go.

"Let me go!" I yelled at the glowing yellow eyes that stared at me angrily.

I attempted to slice off the tentacle with my new aquatic weapon, but another tentacle grabbed it just before I could, preventing me from escaping its grasp. As it pulled me closer to its eyes, they widened. "Wait a minute."

Two more tentacles wrapped around each of my remaining limbs and stretched me apart.

"Let me go! I don't want to be eaten!" I screamed as I struggled.

"You're... Charlie?" the creature asked.

"Yes, now let me go!"

"Not until I ask you this one question of mine."

"Well, I have a question for you, if you don't mind me asking first?"

The creature sighed. "Fine, ask me your question." "Who are you?"

The creature moved its other tentacles over the seagrass, and they released more of the glowing blobs as they surrounded the water, brightening the cave. I watched as the small blobs merged into one another, creating brighter light sources until the creature holding me was revealed.

It was a giant female, squid-looking beast with spines connecting two webbed fins between her head. Her body was a hot pink, and the long tentacles were red, with the inner part of the body where the tentacles connected being webbed. "I am Pearl."

My eyes widened when I remembered the fish

warning me about her. "You're the apex predator of the reef!"

"Oh? So you know me? The creatures of the reef must've told you about me," she said with an unsatisfied tone as she rolled her five eyes.

I noticed one of her eyes was grey and damaged, as if something must've punched through it. Thinking about that, I realised I was face-to-face with Kira's monster who had taken her arm! *That's the Giant Spider Squid!*

Pearl noticed my look of terror and she chuckled. "I love seeing the look of fear. But now, you must answer *my* question: where is the fish?"

My head was unable to process her question, so I just stuttered.

Pearl became impatient and said, "Oh. So, you're giving me the cold shoulder now? I'm positive that you've seen her light. She made those golden pearls that I used to lure my prey!"

I understood now what she meant, but I worried if I told her, she would do something horrible to it! So I pretended I didn't know. "W...what are you talking about?"

Hearing what I asked, Pearl was aggravated, and her five eyes widened, giving a menacing glare. She stretched my limbs more, leaving me in agony.

"*Don't play dumb with me!* The fish is my prey! I must satisfy my hunger! However, the pearls attracted you instead. So you must have some answers for me. Tell me where she is, and I will let you go," she snarled, saliva drifting out of her mouth.

"And if not?" I asked in a painful straining tone, still pretending to be confused.

"Then I will eat you!"

I panicked when she said that. *"You better not! I'll…I'll slice your tongue!"* I looked at the stump of where I had somehow sliced off her tentacle.

Pearl laughed hysterically. "Oh, Charlie, Charlie, Charlie. As a Giant Spider Squid I am, I can forcefully regenerate the missing limbs that you cut off me like this."

The stump of her missing tentacle began shaking, and a new tentacle quickly grew out the same size as all the shorter ones.

I was in great shock at how quickly it grew back that I quietly mumbled to myself, "Well, that's terrifying."

But Pearl heard me and shot a wide grin, showing all of her thin and black razor-sharp teeth. "Good! You should be afraid! Now tell me where the fish is, or you are my little snack."

She moved my limbs together and wrapped the tentacles around me, squeezing me so hard that I couldn't breathe. I wriggled my arm where I had my bladed hand and attempted to cut the tentacles off me. But when I saw my hand, it was back to normal.

I was in big trouble!

"I'm telling you! I don't know who or what the fish is! I am telling the truth!" My voice was weak.

"You are lying! Tell me where she is!" Pearl snapped at me, squeezing me much tighter.

My bones felt like Pearl's strong pressure was

crushing them. I struggled to say a single word, but nothing came out because of how much pain I was in.

Then, I heard the sounds of Atom's propellers in his drone feet, and he shone his flashlight arm in Pearl's eyes, blinding her.

"*My eyes!*" she screamed.

Her tentacles slipped off me, and I could finally breathe again.

Atom bought me some time for me to escape Pearl, and then he followed behind, lighting the way out through the tunnel and out to the open reef.

After escaping that horrid lair of Pearl's, I stopped to catch my breath. I looked at Atom as I panted. "Thanks, Atom."

"Thank me later, Charlie. We need to get back to Chuck before we get in trouble. Dawn is beginning to arrive!"

I looked at the surface of the water and noticed that it was starting to get brighter, so I agreed immediately. "Right! Let's get back to the cenote before we get caught!"

"You can't escape me!" We heard Pearl scream in rage from the cave. Then her five glowing yellow eyes appeared inside the darkness and came for us! I grabbed Atom and swam as quickly as I could to the reef.

As we made our way in, I began feeling a huge amount of energy building in my flippers. I looked and saw bubbles moving around them as my feet glowed white. The energy felt so strong that I could swim forever, maybe even faster.

"What's happening to my feet?" I asked, very confused.

Suddenly, Pearl emerged from the cave. I curled my legs in fright, and yelps escaped our lips. The sudden movement of my legs caused the energy in my flippers to flash.

Pearl heard us and went for us.

As soon as I turned and started kicking my feet, I dashed at super speed through the reef, leaving a trail of bubbles behind, and sand rose in the water.

"*I'm so fast!*" I yelled.

Shocked and also in disbelief, Atom exclaimed, "*That's incredible! But maybe watch where you're going, because we are about to run into corals!*"

I looked ahead and saw we were about to hit a cluster of corals. I reacted quickly and changed direction, avoiding collision. I had to learn how to control my speed as it was new.

We avoided schools of fish and more rocks full of corals as I swam at really great speed.

I looked back and saw Pearl refusing to leave us alone, her mouth wide open and showing her black razor-sharp teeth snapping at us and with some of her tentacles trying to reach us.

I continuously outmanoeuvred obstacles along the way until we reached the Kelp Forest, evading rocks and the really long kelp that was everywhere as we began searching for the cave.

Pearl was still behind us. But as we went further into the biome, some of the kelp around her began to get tangled in her tentacles, slowing her down. Hearing her struggling grunts and growls, we turned and saw that she was stuck, giving us a bit of time to look for the cave. I let go of Atom and we looked in different directions, but we were completely surrounded by kelp.

"Where's the cave?" I exclaimed worriedly.

"Now is not the time to be lost!" Atom's voice cried with fear.

We kept looking around until we heard the sounds of kelp being ripped off the ground. We watched her biting off the tangled kelp from her tentacles and spitting out the chunks. She faced us with her wide and dangerous eyes. We backed away as she approached, growling at us as she got closer. I hugged Atom close to me as my breathing quickened.

"Now I've got you in my sight, and you will be mine!" she snarled.

I looked away and closed my eyes.

But then, all of a sudden, a bright flash of light appeared out of nowhere and blinded Pearl again. "*My eyes! Not again!*"

I opened my eyes and saw her falling backwards as she constantly rubbed at all her eyes. Seeing her stunned, I quickly moved my hands off Atom and tried using my water power to control the flow of the current, successfully pushing her away and out of the Kelp Forest.

After a moment, when everything had calmed and Pearl was gone, my quick, frightened breathing slowed, and I sank down onto the mossy seafloor, closing my eyes as relief filled my body.

"Are you okay?" Atom asked.

"Yeah," I puffed. "Was that it?"

"The light?"

I nodded faintly. "Pearl knows about it. If I'd told her, she would've done something horrible."

"I take your word for it. Is that what that beast's name is?"

"It is. I don't want to be in the water anymore. We need to get back to Chuckboi and tell him what we saw!"

"I agree. Plus, I'm surprised we hadn't been caught yet," Atom replied.

"I wouldn't say that if I were you, dude. I don't want to jinx it," I said.

I got back up and swam to the surface to see where we were as Atom followed me. When my head rose out of the water, I looked around and saw the Oceanic Mountainside, indicating that we weren't far away. I went back under. "We're not far from the cave, follow me."

We both made our way through the Kelp Forest until we finally found the cave. Atom still had his drone's flashlight arm on, and he entered first. Before I joined him, I faced the Kelp Forest one more time and thought about the light that saved us. We had searched everywhere for it, but it was nowhere to be found until we encountered Pearl. Maybe it was too scared to show itself and remained in the shadows. Could the light have followed us, watching us from a distance?

Questions circled my mind, but they quickly disappeared when the mysterious voice in my head spoke. *She's out there! If Pearl must know about my*

She must be hiding from her. Perhaps next time I re-enter the water, I will have another look for her light. But from now on, I have to return to my friends and tell them, and then tell Kira about this. If she found out we were here, we'd be grounded. If we do, remember what I said?

If that is your plan, Mindatar. Then so be it.

Finally, I followed Atom into the cave and made our way back to the cenote.

I rose to the surface to see Atom and Chuckboi again. The light from the ceiling above me filled the cenote. Once Atom lifted up his goggles, the drone shut down and started sinking back down. I quickly caught it and gave it to him, then I got out of the water. I shook my body to get rid of as much water as I could until I changed back to normal.

"What'd you two find? I had to cover your mouth a few times, Atom, because you were screaming," Chuckboi said.

Atom gave him a pitiful look. "I'm sorry. We found the light the second we encountered Kira's monster!"

Hearing this, Chuckboi's eyes sharply widened as he gave us a very worried frown. He came straight to me and checked if I was alright. "Are you hurt, little Marshmallow?"

"I'm fine. She did try to strangle me, but Atom saved me by shining his drone's flashlight in her eyes. We need to get to Kira before she finds out we've been here!"

"Good idea! Let's get out of here!" Atom said.

We headed to the gap and carefully squeezed our way through. Once we reached the other side, I turned to the boys as Atom had gotten out next.

The sky slowly turned blue, signifying it had reached dawn.

"That was close," I sighed.

"Agreed!" Atom replied. "I'm glad we didn't get jinxed."

"Same," I said. "Then things would've been horribly bad if Kira found out we were here."

Chuckboi finally got out last, but his face turned pale as he must've seen something behind me.

Atom and I both looked at him.

"What's wrong, dude?" I asked.

He said nothing but pointed at what was behind me, and I heard someone clear their throat.

Atom turned and yelped, as his face had the same shocked expression as Chuckboi's.

My eyes widened in horror as I recognised who cleared their throat, and slowly turned around, seeing that Kira was there! Her arms were crossed as she glared at us.

Shoot! We're so screwed! I thought.

I laughed nervously and wanted to tell her that I could explain.

But she snapped, "Don't even think about it."

We were too afraid to speak.

"What did I just tell you yesterday?" Kira asked.

Atom answered, "You told us to—"

But Kira cut him off. "That was a rhetorical

question, Atom! I was so specific in telling you to not go back in there! I have already given you a warning and you decide to go back in anyway? Are you deaf?"

I knew I had to explain why we came back, so I spoke. "Kira. It's not what it looks like! If you can just let me explain–"

"I don't want to hear any excuses from you, Charlie! You three are grounded for two days now!"

We were in shock. Grounded for two days now? That was not what we agreed on!

Chuckboi and Atom complained about it.

"If you don't stop complaining, then I will make it a week," Kira threatened.

I was in more shock that I quickly told Atom and Chuckboi to shut up, and they did.

"That's what I thought," she scoffed. She then pointed to the exit of the Oceanic Mountainside and said, "Go to the forest and think about what you've done! *Now!*"

Chapter 4

A punishment

As the sun rose higher in the sky from dawn to morning, me, Atom and Chuckboi headed straight to the forest to think about what we did.

When we eventually got to the forest, we looked for a spot to sit down until we walked to one of the nearby rivers further in the forest, called Akkaperry River.

Akkaperry River is famous for its berry bushes scattered near the river. You could sometimes find Sapphire Melons there; however rarely. The Akkaperry Berries are very delicious to Singanoids, but to some animals, especially reptiles—they cause hallucinations. Akkaperry Berries look like mini roses with white flesh on the inside and taste like sweeter blueberries.

Chuckboi and Atom found a spot to sit down near the river while I decided to go on my own. I crossed the river by hopping over rocks and looked for a place. From behind me, I heard Atom speak softly, "I shouldn't have jinxed it."

I stopped on the middle rock of the running river and turned to him. "It's not your fault, Atom, it's mine."

But he disagreed with me. "No, Charlie, it's that

voice's fault in your head."

Chuckboi agreed.

The voice sighed, knowing it was to blame.

Eventually, I told Atom and Chuckboi that I was going to talk to the voice, and they understood. I crossed to the other side and looked for a spot to sit. I found a tree that stretched high into the sky and thought that was a perfect spot to sit for now. I went to the tree and rested my back against it as I let out a huff of annoyed grief.

"Thanks a lot, voice. Now I'm grounded!"

I am truly sorry, Mindatar, the voice spoke with guilt.

"You should be! If only Kira wasn't there and we had told her in Pollen Village, then she would've believed me! Now she won't let me talk!"

I took a moment to calm down by taking deep breaths through my mouth. "Now, since we are here, why don't you make a proper introduction of yourself, and tell me *why* this light is so important to you?"

As you wish, Mindatar. My name is Orla, a spiritual living guardian of the Deep Spirit Tree in the Twilight Zone. My body is gold and I shine so brightly I could be seen from afar down. I am known by most life in the deep ocean. The light I have asked you to find is one of my young ones that I lost in a storm many months ago. Using my telepathy, I located her and learned she had stumbled onto your island. But it's too shallow for me to reach her myself. She is special for a few reasons. One of them is that she shines like gold, is as bright as a star and as small as a pearl. I call her Lulu, the Golden Starpearl.

I was very intrigued by the name, Golden Starpearl. "'Lulu, the Golden Starpearl'? That phrase you said even sounds catchy."

As I see it. I tried with all my strength to shine my light so she could see me, but she didn't flash back. By looking into your memories, I now see the reason why she didn't.

"So that's why my thoughts weren't feeling like my own, and I kept hearing you," I said.

It was, indeed, me. I was trying to show you my distress for a saviour, and I knew you would think I was an illusion at first, but I'm not; I am a living thing.

I thought of when she said she was a living spiritual guardian, so I asked, "Are you a deep-sea spirit, like Mercy?"

That is not what I mean by 'spiritual'. I mean, I am seen as a legend of the sea who cares for and brings the souls of many species together in my Deep Spirit Tree, from the smallest of fish to the largest of leviathans.

"That's incredible, also very interesting. How?"

I have a symbiotic relationship with Manta Ray Sea Slugs. They act as my servants; they sense a corpse of an animal from really far away. They find the corpse and bring it to me, so its soul is now in salvation. In return, I give them shelter within the branches and food from the corpse, as long as they leave a little behind to sink onto the roots. My Deep

Spirit Tree depends on the essence of the souls and my light for photosynthesis. The harmful spirits within the souls are cleansed and absorbed into the branches, allowing it to spontaneously grow.

Learning this stuff made me smile. "That's amazing, Orla! Now tell me, why do you want Lulu back?"

Lulu is the runt of my spawn. She's very important to me and my sons and daughters. Without her, we will be full of sorrow, and darkness will befall all of us; the same for the creatures of the deep and especially the aquatic people.

I got very interested when I heard her say 'aquatic people', so I asked, "Tell me more about the aquatic people."

The aquatic people are like your people but with scales and fins. They sing to me every time I arrive on their island every three years, and they share their greatest treasures with me, even their scales from their loved ones who passed on. It is a tradition to them. To share my generation, I bring along my young to remember it so they will do the same with theirs when they grow up and protect my Deep Spirit Tree. Lulu, however, is special, and they know it too because she is the youngest and smallest of my spawn. Without her, the tradition would collapse if this continued longer; the people's hearts would be filled with aching darkness as would ours.

A feeling of sympathy filled my body as I

understood what she and the aquatic people would go through if this continued longer. "So that's why you need her, because not only is Lulu important to you and your spawn, but also to the 'aquatic people'?"

Yes. That is why I need your help in returning her to me! Please, Goddess. I need you!

I looked at my knees and thought about it. I may be grounded for two days, but from what I thought, it seemed very urgent for Orla to call for me.

I thought very carefully.

Eventually, I made my decision. "I'll find your lost one."

Oh, I greatly bless you with my bliss!

"Let me get back to my boys, and I'll make a plan."

As you wish, dear Mindatar.

I got up and walked back to Akkaperry River, where I saw Atom throwing small pebbles into the water as Chuckboi watched, holding an Akkaperry Snapperfish he must've caught from the water.

Akkaperry Snapperfish is one of Chuckboi's favourite fish. Commonly, he just calls them Snapper or Snapperfish.

Dragadillos—or as Atom scientifically referred to them as *Armoured Wyandoocaahnha*—were believed to swallow their food whole while also having the ability to store objects in a stomach pouch separated from their digestive system. The pouch allows none of its corrosive enzymes to enter. But if a little does get inside, it is immediately absorbed and secreted back into the stomach. Atom also learned from Chuckboi that the females store their one egg in their stomach pouches to incubate it with their body temperature and must lay in the sun if their bodies are too cold. Eventually, before the egg is ready to hatch, they cough it up.

When the boys saw me, Atom put another pebble he had picked up back on the ground, and Chuckboi brought the live Akkaperry Snapperfish into his mouth, slurping it down with one gulp.

"I didn't have breakfast," he said. He belched with his mouth closed, puffing his cheeks like a balloon.

"How did you and the voice go with your conversation?" Atom asked, tilting his head towards Chuckboi.

"She's given me a proper introduction about herself and has told me why the light is so important to her," I answered.

"Why is it so important to her?" Atom asked.

I told them everything Orla had told me, and Atom seemed very intrigued when I mentioned the aquatic people. But I said that I would explain it to him later and told him what was most important. "She does need my help," I added. "If I don't return the runt back to her, she and her spawn would suffer with darkness and grief, and the tradition of the aquatic people will collapse if it continues longer. I have to go back in."

"But we're grounded for two days and we can't go back into the cenote," Chuckboi mentioned.

"I never said I would go back there. I'll wait until nightfall, then leave from our ship, because this will give me the advantage to find her lost one in the darkness," I said.

That is a great plan! Orla spoke in my mind, impressed.

Chuckboi and Atom's eyes met again and they pondered.

Finally, Atom answered, "Count us in! We won't let you do this alone. I'll use my drone to help! Team C.C.A!" He picked up his sleeping drone that was lying on his left and lifted it in the air.

"You really do like making these acronyms up, don't you, Atom?" Chuckboi asked him.

Atom put his drone back down as his cheeks turned red and he answered shyly, "Yeah, I do, Chucky."

Chuckboi wrapped his arm under Atom's head and gave him a playful noogie

"You're cute, not gonna lie," he cackled.

"Heh, same for you, bro," Atom replied as Chuckboi let go of him.

You probably didn't know that I'm not the only one who has a desire for Chuckboi; Atom likes him, too.

Of course, you might be thinking: *'But if Atom likes your boyfriend, does that make you jealous?'* or *'Why does he like him when he's different?'*

My answer to those questions is, why wouldn't he?

Also, I'm honestly not jealous at all; they're both my homies, and I'm extremely proud of who they are. They have the right to love each other as bros, too, and even love each other more than just bros. I respect everyone's differences and personalities.

Now that we were in a secret team, we headed back to our ship.

Chapter 5

Getting our feet wet again

When we returned home, Atom and I immediately started getting ourselves ready for the journey we were about to undertake.

Atom got to his lab and began making better modifications to the drone, and I watched. He carefully tore apart small mechanics and put them aside to modify with his tools and machines.

As he did, I exited the lab and headed to my art room to watch the ocean horizon for a bit from the small window beside my art desk. I took a deep breath, knowing the journey me and Atom were about to face was going to be deep in the ocean.

Then I heard soft knocking from the entrance of my art room. "May I come in?"

I turned and saw that it was Stephenie with a puzzled look in her eyes.

I nodded, allowing her to enter my room.

"What is Genshi doing?" she asked.

I approached her. "Me and Atom are on a mission to find something in the waters of the Oceanic Mountainside. There's a voice in my head telling me all of this."

"A voice? When did you start hearing it?" she asked.

"Yesterday. She told me she was far in the deep ocean and had lost one of her younglings in a storm. She needs me to find it and return it to her," I explained.

Stephenie's eyes grew wide, and she covered her mouth as she gasped.

"I know, it's horrible. But we have to do this for her and for the voice's friends' sake and save their tradition from collapsing," I added.

She understood. "Be careful out there, Char'i. This one will be nothing you have faced before. I'm also glad Genshi is coming with you, too."

"It's nothing Atom and I have ever faced, but we have each other's backs," I replied.

This female Singanoid is very understanding!

She understands everyone, even if other people think it's crazy. I'm lucky to have her in my team.

You should be, Mindatar!

And I am!

Soon, Stephenie left my art room. Before walking through the corridor, she placed her hand on the side of the doorway, glanced at me and said, "Be safe and good luck, Goddess. Bless this voice and her friends with your protection."

I nodded, smiling more widely, touched by her positivity.

Finally, she left.

I stared at the doorway for a bit before thinking about going to Atom's lab again to see what he was up to with the drone. So, I headed out of my room.

But just at the doorway, I saw something blue in the corner of my right eye and got so frightened that I jumped and yelped. "Holy…Mercy! Please don't do that!"

"Sorry! Did I scare you?"

It turned out to be Sandy, who must've been passing by or something.

I took a few deep breaths until I finally said, "Ya think?"

"I'm very sorry. I overheard you saying that you were going to the ocean to find a creature?" she asked.

I nodded.

"Let me come with you! You are gonna need someone like me, especially in case we get separated or somethin'. My senses could really be of good use," she said with a confident smile.

I thought about that for a moment.

What do you think, dear Mindatar?

I'm thinking.

Finally, I agreed that Sandy could come with us. "You're in!"

Sandy was super pleased when I told her. "Wesome! (*Awesome!*) I'm ready when you are, Alpha!"

I nodded, then replied, "Let me talk to Atom first." I headed to Atom's lab as she stood, watching me enter.

Atom had his goggles over his eyes and was working at his desk with the torn-apart drone, adding and replacing bits here and there to fix it.

I didn't want to disturb him, so I looked around and saw a stack of unused blue and white paper in the corner to the right of his lab.

The blue paper he uses for making blueprints and the white paper either for notes or to print or draw anatomic pictures of organic functions or hypotheses.

I approached, took one piece of white paper and picked up a pen that rested on his biomechanical desk next to them, where he experiments with chemicals using vials and test tubes, and wrote '*Sandy is going to join us in our journey*' in Hybrainian. I then walked back to Atom and slipped it carefully into his right hand. He noticed the note, stopped what he was doing, grabbed it and lifted up his goggles to read. He then turned to me and nodded with a soft smile.

I returned the nod, and then I asked, "How far have you got with improving the drone?"

"Just a few more moments. I'll let you know when I'm done. In the meantime, why don't you hone your water skills?" he suggested.

I thought that was a good idea. So I left the lab, and walked through the corridor as Sandy decided to follow me until I walked up the stairs and into the shipyard. But when I did, I saw Chuckboi staring out into the ocean horizon.

Seeing him there, my heart began to race, and I let out a sigh of adoration.

"I think you and Chuck would make a great couple," Sandy whispered.

Hearing her say that, I covered my face as it heated up. "Shut up, Sandy!"

Chuckboi must've heard me as he turned to us and softly chuckled when he saw me cover my face. A few seconds later, I felt him grabbing my arms and moving them off my face before placing his hands under my chin, tilting my face up to his. I looked into his eyes as his face turned pink, and he gently rubbed my cheeks with his thumbs.

My embarrassment faded away, and I closed my eyes, enjoying the feeling.

"Why were you so embarrassed earlier?" he asked.

"It's nothing," I replied.

"Alright, little Marshmallow. How are you feeling about this new journey ahead of you?"

I opened my eyes again. "A little nervous, since this is nothing I've ever faced before."

"It's going to be okay, Charlie. Remember that Atom will be there for you. I know it feels different from the other journeys that you've had, but I believe in you like always. Stay strong, little Marshmallow!"

I smiled at him.

Such strong confidence he has in you. Listen to him! Orla said in my mind.

Chuckboi brought me to his chest and wrapped his arms around me, giving me a gentle squeeze.

"I'm coming along with them, too!" Sandy added.

"That's great, Sandy!" Chuckboi said.

Eventually, he let go of me, and I said to him, "I'm just going to hone my water skills."

"I'll watch you!"

I smiled more widely when he said that. Then, I walked to the ledge where Chuckboi originally was, climbed on top, looked down at the water, and jumped off, splashing in.

I transformed into my water form and began honing my skills by trying new movements.

I remember earlier when my hand turned into a weapon when I encountered Pearl, and I wanted to try and practise bringing it out. So, I moved my hand close to my chest, held it for a few seconds, and then quickly swung it out.

Nothing happened.

I looked at my hand with disappointment, but I didn't give up. I thought of closing my fist and then swinging it out. So, I did that. I closed my fist, brought it close to my chest, and waited a few seconds. As I did, I noticed the pattern of my hand slowly change into a more complex one. Finally, I swung it outward, and it changed into a small blade!

"There we go!" I said to myself, pleased.

I moved my hand around with great interest and thought of testing the sharpness by gently moving one of my fingers over it. But little did I know, it cut my finger, and I quickly moved it off. "Ouch! That's sharper than I thought!"

Then, unexpectedly, the pain from my cut finger quickly faded away, and a line of blue light surrounded the cut, quickly healing it until it was gone!

My eyes widened as I couldn't believe what I had just seen! "Do I have regenerative powers? That will definitely come in handy! I wonder what other abilities I haven't uncovered yet? I can already control water, turn my hand into a blade, control the currents, talk to sea creatures, I have super speed… what else?"

Those are all your abilities, as far as I know,

too.

"I guess. Well, I just need to wait until nightfall now. Maybe after honing my abilities out of the water to pass the time," I said.

I headed to the shore near the dock the Singanoids built for us earlier in the year and continued honing my skills by controlling the water. Chuckboi came to the other side of the shipyard to continue watching me as I did.

Watching the water rise and magically float in the air felt so soothing that I closed my eyes. Something about water reminded me of my past, something Mercy, the Mother of the Wisps, taught me when I bloomed into this world. I can still remember her soft, ancient voice when she told me water was important to all the life I had created in Hybrainia. To the Singanoid Race in ancient times, water symbolised regeneration, purity, peace, strangeness and song.

I smiled as it all came back to me and said under my breath, "If only you were here, Mercy."

The Mother of the Wisps brings you tranquillity. It's a shame that she's gone, Orla said in my head.

"Mercy isn't gone; she's somewhere hidden," I replied.

My mistake.

Eventually, when I thought I had honed my water skills enough after an hour or two, I slowly and gently moved the floating water down until it was absorbed back into the sea. Then I went to the ladder and climbed up into the shipyard, where Chuckboi remained, and we both headed to the other side of the shipyard to watch the distant ocean.

A few more hours later, the sun began to set, and the stars slowly appeared in the sky.

It was almost time for me, Atom and Sandy to start our journey of finding the lost light.

Me and Sandy, and Chuckboi, who still stayed by my side, waited for Atom to sort some things out. I was back to normal, as the water I carried on me had dried up during the sunlight hours.

I felt nervous about starting this new journey as I had never been in the far waters before, I've only crossed them with a Long-Finned Leviathan. Sandy seemed nervous too as she was breathing very deeply.

Finally, Atom came up with his drone paired to his goggles; behind him followed everyone else, including Stephenie, Violet and Eric, who had soft looks on their faces and had come to say their goodbyes.

Violet approached me and gave me the first hug. "Sandy told us about your journey. We will keep this secret safe with us. We promise, Alpha."

Hearing her say that, my worry faded and I knew I could trust them. Usually, Eric and Violet weren't really good at keeping secrets, but this was different.

Violet finally let go and moved away as Bucky approached me, dragging my Diamond Rapier on the wooden deck. When he was close enough, he put it down, huffing and puffing as it was heavy for him.

"I brought your weapon, Charlie," he panted, "You will need it, won't you?"

I knelt down and moved my hand to cup his small cheek. "Thank you, buddy. But I won't need it for this journey; my hand turns into a weapon so sharp that it cuts through flesh, even with the smoothest and most gentle touch," I replied.

His eyes sparkled. "That's amazing! But won't you need your Diamond Rapier?"

"Not for this journey, dude. I promise when we get home, I'll tell you everything about it."

Bucky smiled even more, then came and wrapped his little arms around me. I wrapped mine around him and gave him a gentle squeeze.

"Be careful out there, Charlie. I love you," he said softly.

"I love you too, buddy," I replied.

This young male Gippypuppy has a very strong bond with you. He seems to see you as family.

He does. I protect him with all of my heart. I let no one touch him unless I trust them.

That sounds just like what a mother would do.

Eventually, Bucky and I let go of each other, and I faced Chuckboi, knelt back up, and wrapped my arms around him. My head was on his chest, and his arms wrapped around me.

"Be careful out there, little Marshmallow," he whispered.

"Always will. We'll come back in one piece," I replied.

Finally, it was time for me, Sandy, and Atom to begin the journey.

I walked to the ledge that faced the water below and turned to my friends as Atom handed Sandy his drone before she followed me.

"Ee ou oon! (See you soon!)" I said in the Hybrainian language and pointed at Chuckboi before shaping my hands to a heart and placing it near my chest.

"Ee ou oon, Charlie (See you soon, Charlie)," Chuckboi said back as he did the same back for me.

I turned back to the water, took a deep breath and jumped, splashing in. Bubbles rose around me and my body changed form. I heard another splash from my right and knew that it was Sandy and Atom's drone that he would soon control.

"We're right behind you, Charlie! Where do we need to go?" Sandy asked.

"Let me speak to Orla," I replied. I then spoke to Orla with my inner voice. *Where do you think Lulu may be?*

She's still near the Oceanic Mountainside. Please go there and find her! I hope she's alright!

We will find her, Orla. I promise.

"The Oceanic Mountainside," I answered Sandy.

That seemed to surprise her. "Isn't that where Kira lost her arm to a monster?"

"That's not important right now; we must do this for Orla. Let's go!" I started swimming in the direction of the Oceanic Mountainside as Sandy followed me, carrying Atom's drone in her wings until it started coming alive as Atom, back at home, operated it.

Chapter 6

Critters in the Kelp Forest

When we finally made it to the waters of the Oceanic Mountainside, we stopped, and I turned to my friends. "The light could be anywhere in the Kelp Forest. Let's split up and keep our eyes peeled. We don't know what will be lurking in here, so stay alert. Yell if you find something," I instructed.

"You know it!" Sandy replied.

"Got it!" Atom replied.

Sandy released him from her wings, and then they went their separate ways. As they disappeared into the kelp, I closed my hand and swung so it turned into its blade form, in case I ran into any threats, and finally went my own way.

I was certain that it could be somewhere around here. As I searched, I asked Orla, "So, Orla, what does Lulu look like?"

She is a small and round goldfish with a really long tail fin. You will be able to find her if you catch a glimpse of her light.

"Got it. A small, round goldfish with a long tail fin. I'll keep a lookout," I replied.

I continued searching through the Kelp Forest, even checking under rocks and small tunnels, until I saw one with a gold light bursting from a nearby tunnel. I came and inspected it to see if it was there. But it wasn't. There were only gold-coloured tiny spots in the tunnel and a green crab that had awoken by my appearance. It immediately crawled out and attempted to nip me with its large claws, but I just managed to avoid it.

"Hey! What's your problem?" the crab exclaimed angrily in a high-pitched voice.

"Sorry! I'm just looking for a light. I thought that was it in your tunnel. I didn't mean to disturb you."

The crab crossed its claws. "A light, eh? Well, I didn't see anything here tonight. But maybe talk to the Whisperer of the Reef; he lives in the reef nearby and is such a kind guy! He might know."

"The Whisperer of the Reef? Who is he?" I asked, curious as to who that was. Could he have answers as to where Lulu may be?

Before the crab answered, a high-pitched sneeze was heard nearby, and I turned to where it came from and saw rays of light escaping from the kelp.

The crab saw, too, and then asked me, "Is that it?"

"I think so."

It is! It's Lulu!

The rays began to fade.

Where is she going? Please follow her!

I left the crab for the light and moved the kelp out of my way to follow it.

"If you find the whisperer, say hi for me!" the crab yelled as I left its domain.

I followed the moving light until it went over some

mossy rocks, and it stopped in the middle of a small open area in the kelp.

I shrank down and hid behind the rocks and slightly squinted my eyes to see what the source of the light was.

There was a long, blue and beautiful tail with three little orange tips around its body and two small blue fins in the front. It looked like a round, tiny goldfish.

Is that Lulu, Orla?

Yes, it is Lulu! Oh, thank Hybrainia, she's alright! Wait…what is that in front of her?

I noticed two glowing teal eyes and blue fins emerging from the kelp and staring directly at Lulu.

Seeing its familiar appearance, I gasped in surprise. It was the creature that was watching me from the dark cave!

Lulu softly gasped at the creature's appearance as she froze. As it slowly approached her until her light reflected on its body, the creature was revealed to be a male Singanoid!

The Singanoid was bald and had two colours: turquoise for most of his body, while his lower legs, forearms and hands were blue! There were fins on his cheeks, and he was wearing pants made of kelp and seagrass! Scales covered his shoulders and forearms.

I watched in awe as he slowly moved his hands under Lulu, softly comforting her with his gentle words. The rest he whispered, but I couldn't hear what he was saying. The Singanoid was able to calm her down, and she made herself comfortable in his big hands.

"That's a Singanoid?" I said quietly.

Suddenly the Singanoid's head rose, followed by his fins on his cheeks as if he must have heard me. I went under the rocks before I was spotted.

"Who's there?" he said as he looked around, confused. "Don't be shy! It's okay! Show yourself."

But I remained hidden as I began to breathe rapidly.

"Your breathing sounds fast. I won't hurt you, I promise," he said with a soft expression.

I covered my mouth with my hands, and repeatedly thought, *Breathe, Charlie, stay calm! Stay hidden, and he won't find you!*

Why are you frightened? What is he even doing here?

Did you hear what he said? He can hear me breathing! What do you mean by that last question? What is he?

He's a Mersinganoid; one of the aquatic people! He's not supposed to be here.

Before I could speak, I was caught in the Mersinganoid's giant blue hands. I froze like stone as I was brought towards him. His hands slowly opened to see me as I remained silent and looked him in the eyes.

His eyes widened and his grin grew wider, excited. "Hey… it's you from earlier! You've arrived at our home at last!"

He noticed I was scared, so he slowly moved one of his hands apart from the other that held me. I covered my face, worried about what the Mersinganoid was about to do.

But then I felt one of his fingers caressing my head.

"It's okay, Mindatar. Don't be afraid; I won't hurt you, I promise. Everything will be okay. Take your time, little Goddess."

Hearing those words come out of his mouth, I realised that he wasn't much of a threat. I began to control my breathing. After a deep breath, I felt a lot better. I lowered my hands from my eyes and faced him again.

"There you go," he said, "See? It's okay. Even as a mighty Goddess and protector of Hybrainia, you're very delicate, just like that little, shiny fish."

That made me remember Lulu, who was behind the Mersinganoid. I hopped off his hand and swam past the left side of him, seeing Lulu still there. I approached as I grew back to my normal size. But then the Mersinganoid grabbed my leg, stopping me from reaching her.

"Don't come too close to her, Mindatar; she's very fragile," he told me.

I was surprised that he could understand Lulu's emotions.

Orla then told me that the fins on his cheeks act as emotional sensors, which allow him to detect the exact emotion a creature feels in front of him.

When he must've found Lulu just after you, she was scared, and he knew exactly what to do. Can you tell him why you're here?

I nodded at Orla, and the Mersinganoid thought I was agreeing not to get too close to Lulu that he let go of my leg. I turned to him and opened my mouth to tell him why I was there, but I was interrupted by two familiar voices.

"You found it, Charlie!"

"Charlie! Get the creature before *that* creature does!"

It was Atom and Sandy who had emerged from the kelp.

Because of their unexpected presence, Lulu screamed and froze, and the Mersinganoid was so startled that his pupils were constricted. He rushed to Lulu and shielded her in his arms as he hissed at them, thinking they were threats. The scales on his forearms and shoulders flared up.

Seeing this new creature who was defending Lulu, Atom gasped in amazement.

But Sandy hissed back, thinking he was also a threat. She went straight for him to attack, but I reacted quickly and blocked Sandy from attacking the Mersinganoid.

"Sandy, no! Don't hurt him!" I yelled.

Sandy stared at me in shock. "Charlie? What are you doing? That thing has got the light that we're searching for! He could be a threat to it!" She attempted to swim past me and attack, but I used my water powers to push her back. When she managed to control herself after being pushed by the current I used, she shook her head and growled like a tiger.

"He's not a threat," I exclaimed, "he calmed me down and proved he wasn't going to hurt me!"

"But he could've been playing a trick on you! I don't trust him, especially when he comes near you!" Sandy argued.

I wasn't happy with her attitude towards the innocent Mersinganoid. "He wasn't trying to hurt me!"

Me and Sandy growled at each other furiously until Atom broke us up. "Girls! Let's not be nasty about it. We can kindly ask him to give us the little fish. Observe."

We both watched him as he approached the Mersinganoid as he growled at him. I wasn't comfortable with Atom's plan.

I don't have a comfortable feeling about your friend's idea either. He could scare him even more! Orla said worriedly in my mind.

Atom cleared his throat. "We, land creatures, must obtain the little light you are defending to take back home!"

We were confused as to why Atom was talking like a caveman to the Mersinganoid, even the Mersinganoid was confused.

"Atom? He can speak our language," I reminded him, my hands on my hips.

"Oh, sorry, I didn't know," he said, smacking his head with his metallic arm, "Can we have that little fish you are defending? We are trying to take it back to where it came from…please?"

The Mersinganoid refused as he moved back from Atom a tiny bit.

Atom swam closer. "Please?"

The Mersinganoid still refused.

"*Pleeeease?*" Atom said again, becoming very desperate.

The Mersinganoid hissed at him again.

"I know! It may look this way, but we're friends, not foes! We just need to take it back to where it came from. *Please?*" Atom asked again, hoping that the Mersinganoid would give Lulu to him this time.

The Mersinganoid glanced at her in his hands for a moment. "I'm sorry about this," he whispered to her.

Then he quickly shoved her into his mouth!

Shocked gasps filled our lungs at what had just happened!

"*Nooo!*" Atom screamed in terror.

Lulu! Orla cried so loudly that I grasped my head and furiously closed my eyes. "Orla!" I exclaimed.

Oh, I apologise!

The Mersinganoid then looked at me and quickly swam straight to me, nabbed my arm and escaped into the kelp, taking me with him.

"*Charlie!*" Sandy and Atom both yelled in distress as we disappeared into the Kelp Forest.

Chapter 7

The Whisperer of the Reef

I didn't know where the Mersinganoid was taking me and Lulu. He covered his mouth with one hand to prevent her from getting out, and he held my arm tightly as we went further into the Kelp Forest.

We went past rocks, arches, and even a place where there was an underwater flowery area with huge pink-petalled flowers with thick dark-magenta stems. By how fast the Mersinganoid was going, he almost created a current behind him; the huge flowers flipped upside down, revealing that they weren't just ordinary aquatic flowers but jellyfish!

They opened their dotted eyes because they were suddenly surprised by the strong current the Mersinganoid made.

One of them caught us in their tentacles. "What's the matter, Whisperer?" it said, noticing the Mersinganoid's distress.

My eyes widened when I heard the word 'whisperer'.

Could that mean that the Mersinganoid was the Whisperer of the Reef? I remembered earlier that the green crab mentioned them before I found Lulu. If he must be the Whisperer of the Reef, then why do they call him that?

As I thought about it, the Mersinganoid let go of my arm and pointed to where we came from. He used sign language despite being unable to speak due to keeping Lulu inside his mouth.

A shock ran down our spines when I heard Sandy's loud cry, full of rage. Then Sandy dashed out of the kelp with Atom holding on to her spines tightly. When she saw us, she yelled at the Mersinganoid, "*Give us back our leader!*"

Just when she and Atom were about to dash for me, the Mersinganoid's arms wrapped around me and then the petal-like tentacles of the jellyfish did as we began to rise from the seabed and away from them.

They watched us as the jellyfish took us away.

"*You really thought you could get away with Alpha, huh?*" Sandy stretched her wings and charged right at us.

As she got closer, the Mersinganoid unwrapped his arms, pushed me slightly down and spat Lulu at them. Lulu's light was so bright up close that I had to cover my eyes to avoid being blinded. Sandy and Atom were too slow to react and were both blinded by her light.

"*My eyes!*" Atom cried.

"*This is worse than being colour-blind!*" Sandy screamed.

I was lucky to cover my eyes, but I couldn't see what was going on. I moved my hands away until I noticed Atom and Sandy both moving away from me; the Mersinganoid was down there, too, grabbing Lulu and bringing her back to me, as well as the jellyfish that held me. He swam onto the creature's head for a ride as we went further through the kelp and eventually to the reef that me and Atom had explored before.

I watched in awe, seeing all of the bioluminescence of the corals that swayed and moved gently with the soft current.

As we passed the corals and further into the reef than we had explored, we were taken to a shallow sinkhole.

Few corals surrounded the hole, while some were on the sand and rocks that hugged the walls. At the back was a giant pink coral that looked like a flower facing down and closed with something pink glowing inside. Its roots twirled and went under or over the sand and looped over its own roots.

I was fascinated.

When we reached the sand, the Mersinganoid got off the flower-looking jellyfish, and it gently let me go. I slowly landed on my hands and knees on the sand and looked around, my eyes sparkling. I approached the nearest exposed root and stared at it for a moment before placing my hand on it.

But just when I did, the veins of the root lit up red, and I quickly moved my hand off, startled. Then I looked at the Mersinganoid as he pressed his forehead onto the jellyfish. "Thank you, Bella, for taking us back to my nest."

"With pleasure, Whisperer," it replied.

Eventually, he moved back and watched as it swam away to the Kelp Forest.

I began to worry about Sandy and Atom still being

in there, stunned by Lulu's light. But my mood changed when the Mersinganoid turned and faced me with Lulu in his hands.

He looked at her for a second, then released her, and she quickly rushed and hid behind me, trembling in fear.

Oh, Lulu! You're okay! I'm here, Lulu! Orla exclaimed in my head.

Orla? I don't think she can hear you.

I'm just so relieved she wasn't swallowed!

Why would he do that? He was only trying to defend her!

I believe that is true.

I snapped back when I noticed the Mersinganoid approaching me. He went down onto his knees in front of me.

I stared at him, at a loss for words. Finally, I asked, "Why did you bring me here?"

"Because now that you've arrived in my reef, I am truly honoured that I wanted to give you my blessing," he answered as he went down with his hands in front of his head, and his cheek fins began vibrating, flashing in bright aqua. "Oh, dear, great and mighty Mindatar of this world, with me blessed upon your arrival, I willingly bless you back with my prayers, respect and my welcoming for you to my reef," he prayed.

I didn't know what to say, so I smiled at him.

When he rose back up, he tilted over to his left to see Lulu behind me. I glanced at her, too, but she swam further down behind my back to hide.

I paused for a long time. Finally, I said to the

Mersinganoid, "I've seen you before, back in the cave when I discovered my aquatic form! You were watching me! Who are you?"

"Everyone in the reef calls me 'Whisperer' or 'Whisperer of the Reef,' but you can call me Jasper."

"Jasper?" I said. I wondered if he was the same creature who drew those pictures back in the cave. So I asked him, "Are you the one who also drew those pictures in the cave?"

He nodded. "I was."

"From what I'm guessing, because a few of them had, like, a weird creature, is it…like…some sort of squid?" I asked curiously.

"Yes, she's a squid."

After Jasper spoke, we heard stretching noises from the giant flower behind me. I turned my body around, and Lulu hid her face on my chest. I held her with one hand as the petals slowly opened.

A half-pink and teal ball was revealed inside. Between the ball were two small dark blue antennas and a long blue, wavy-like back fin.

The ball slowly sank down and landed on the sand by two blue-tipped and dark pink-tipped tentacles. It walked towards us until it stopped in front of me and moved its body until the teal was on top and the pink was on the bottom, and two eyes emerged. The eyes were wide; the irises were blue and shaped like the head of a spear. The pupils were straight black lines, and a wide-open grin popped onto the creature's face. Then the creature hopped, and another smaller set of tentacles emerged as it floated above the sand, staring at me.

I jumped with a surprised yelp.

A Jelly-Capped Squid? She's also not meant to be here! Orla exclaimed.

You seem to know these sea creatures a lot more than I do! I said with my inner voice.

"Sorry! I didn't mean to startle you!" The creature moved her blue-tipped tentacles over her cheeks and showed a look of concern in her eyes.

"It's fine," I replied.

Jasper chuckled softly. "Goddess, this is Jayjay, my best friend."

Jayjay nodded. "It's me! I'm truly honoured that you have come to our reef! I bless you with my prayers, respect and welcoming upon your arrival."

"I thank you. But I need to tell you both that I'm here for a reason," I said.

"Go ahead. What is it you're worried about?" Jasper replied.

Before I could tell them why I was there, we suddenly heard a voice nearby. "Little creature! Where are you? Come out, come out, wherever you are! I just want a little bite!"

We all gasped.

"Pearl's coming! Jayjay, hide them!" Jasper exclaimed quietly.

Lulu panicked because of what Pearl said, and she began to cry.

As Pearl's voice grew closer, I began to panic, thinking that if she saw me with Lulu, we'd be done for!

Then Jayjay wrapped my hips with her blue-tipped

tentacles, took me to the giant aquatic flower, and put Lulu and me inside.

"Sshh," she said.

I nodded before the petals closed on us.

I slightly moved one of the petals with one hand to see what was going on, and I saw Pearl had finally appeared as she sat on the edge of the sinkhole with two of her tentacles resting on her cheeks. She grinned widely at Jasper and Jayjay with her sharp black teeth.

Jasper swam up to her eye height while Jayjay fearfully hid behind him.

I felt Lulu wriggling out of my hand and I quickly closed the hole, preventing her from peeking through.

"Lulu, no, we'll be noticed," I whispered.

"Lulu?" she said, pointing at herself with her tiny blue fin, wondering if that was her name.

"Yes, that's your name, Lulu," I answered.

Her eyes sparkled, amazed that she had learned her name for the first time. She then pointed at me and asked, "You name?"

"I'm Charlie Neon Imagination, nice to meet you."

She waved at me. "Hi."

"Why, hello there, Jasper and Jayjay," I heard Pearl say.

I carefully moved the petal to make a peeping hole again. Lulu wanted to have a look, but I kept her away. "Lulu, don't peek through the hole. You don't want to be eaten, do you?" I whispered.

She shook her body with a worried look.

"That's what I thought, just stay quiet, okay?"

She nodded.

"What do you want, Pearl?" I heard Jasper ask Pearl in an unhappy tone, his arms crossed over his chest.

"Oh, Jasper, the Whisperer of the Reef, my dear friend," she said as she was about to cup his right cheek.

Jasper bit her, and she quickly moved her tentacle away. "Ouch! Chill!"

"Don't ever touch me, and we are not friends!" Jasper exclaimed with a hiss.

Pearl attempted to shake her tentacle in the water, but it just wobbled and floated as if it couldn't move. When she looked at Jasper again, she scoffed, and her five eyes blinked one at a time. "Paralysis? Pathetic! I have more tentacles that I can still use, you little, idiotic Fishman."

Hearing what Pearl said, I was surprised. *I didn't know Jasper has a bite that causes paralysis!* I thought.

All Mersinganoids have that to keep their threats away, Orla explained in my head.

Right.

"You still haven't answered my question, you big, idiotic kraken."

Yeah! Teach her a lesson, Jasper!

I was on the verge of laughing the oxygen out of my lungs when he called her that.

Oh, my! Orla sounded shocked.

But she deserved it!

But soon, I calmed down when I heard familiar laughter and snorting, which angered Pearl more so that she brought two other tentacles in front of her, holding Sandy and Atom in each one!

"*Quiet, you two!*" she snarled at them.

Sandy and Atom stopped laughing and were frightened.

I gasped in shock, "Sandy! Atom!"

Your friends have been captured! Orla exclaimed.

Pearl growled angrily at Jasper. "*I am not a kraken! I am a Giant Spider Squid! Get it right, you little shrimp!*"

Jasper was shocked to see them in Pearl's grasp and she was threatening them.

"Let them go! Tell us what you want!" he begged.

Pearl took a moment to calm down.

"Well, I'm glad you asked. Have either of you, by any chance, found a little, shiny fish in this reef? Tell me where she is and I will let these two go," she said in a menacing tone as she moved Atom and Sandy closer to Jasper.

"Don't tell her, please!" Sandy stammered to him.

"Shut it!" Pearl yelled at Sandy. "Tell me where the little fish is, Jasper, or else these two will get it."

Jasper and Jayjay froze, unsure of what to do, while I watched in shock.

Then, slowly, my hands started to shake, and my breathing roughened as my face started heating up. Lulu looked at me and slowly swam away from me, not knowing what was happening.

Charlie? Are you okay? Orla asked worriedly.

I'm not just going to stand here and watch my friends get hurt, Orla! I am going to teach Pearl a lesson about holding my friends and threatening them!

I used my power to push the flower's petals up in front of me. Then I charged right at Pearl before she even noticed me, and rammed my head extremely hard above her eyes, sending her flying backwards and releasing my friends before crashing into a rock point behind her back.

Sandy took in a massive gulp of oxygen now that she and Atom were free.

I approached them. "Sandy! Atom! You guys okay?"

"Yes, thank you, Charlie. We're so glad we found you! Where's the fish?" Sandy asked worriedly.

Atom agreed.

Before I answered, I heard Lulu approaching me, panting in a high-pitched tone. I turned to her and moved my hands for her to lay down on and catch her breath. "Oh, don't worry, Sandy; she's safe."

Sandy and Atom swam around me to have a look.

"Woah! You definitely weren't kidding about it. That is the shiniest fish I've ever seen in my entire life," Atom said, fascinated.

"I may have been in the Kelp Forest with Barbara, looking for pearls and shells, but I've never ever seen a fish like this before," Sandy said.

"Pear...gone?" Lulu asked me as she panted.

"Yes, Lulu, I kept her away and saved my own friends. Are you okay?"

She nodded. "Mhm."

"That's great. You're in good hands, Lulu; you can trust us."

Lulu smiled widely, then swam to my forehead and

gently pressed hers just below my symbols.

I'm so glad she is okay. She has learned to trust you and now knows that she is safe with you, Orla said in my mind.

"Her name is Lulu? How do you know her name?" Jayjay asked as she and Jasper approached us.

But Sandy quickly swam in front of me, spreading her wings and hissing at Jayjay, frightening her so much that she swam behind Jasper's back again. When Sandy saw his face, she growled more angrily at him. "*You!*"

She doesn't sound very pleased to see him again, Orla said worriedly.

Sandy gets very tense and protective. But hopefully, she'll get over it.

It doesn't look like it, Charlie.

"*You took our Alpha! Now you're gonna pay, you blue fiend!*" Sandy's yelling startled Lulu, so she hid her face on my skin. Before Sandy could do anything to harm Jasper and Jayjay, I grabbed her shoulder. "Sandy, no! Just calm down!"

She moved her wings slightly down and turned to me. Then she put her hands together in front of her three gills on her face and deeply took a breath with her eyes closed. She opened her eyes again, dropped hands down and gave me a look. "Alpha, no offence, but please give me one reason why I should get a grip."

"They meant no harm, and you're being too tense over them. Jasper took me and Lulu because he only wanted to give me his blessing. Plus, he's blue and turquoise. Just breathe, Sandy."

Sandy looked at the sand under her for a moment, then took slow breaths. Finally, she let out a deep sigh. "You're right. I must've been very tense over them. I should apologise to them."

I smiled with a nod and slipped my hand off her shoulder. She approached Jasper and Jayjay and said, "I'm sorry I called you a fiend. I was just very tense. We just got off the wrong fin, and I just should've taken a step back and not have been threatening you critters. We just needed to return that little fish to where she belongs and for her mother's sake."

Lulu picked up something Sandy said, and she turned around and stared at her.

Jasper nodded and smiled. "It's okay, I sensed you were feeling tense at the start, and I understand that you just wanted to protect her. You startled me, though, and that was also why I took Lulu and Charlie away from you."

"Mama? She say mama?" Lulu said to me.

I gently moved Lulu down from my forehead and her eyes met mine. "You heard her, Lulu. We are going to take you home, back to Mama Orla!"

Her eyes began to sparkle, and she made happy noises. "Mama…Orwa?"

I nodded with a grin. "Yes! Back to Mama Orla!"

Lulu then zoomed around me, squealing and giggling with joy. I couldn't stop laughing until she finally swam to my chest and rubbed her forehead to show me how grateful she was.

"Such a bright little infant," Atom said.

I agreed. "We are going to take her home."

"Can we come?" Jayjay asked. She must've overheard what I said and wanted to come along with us.

But I shook my head at her. "Oh, no way, Jayjay. I'm sorry, but you and Jasper cannot come with us. I don't want to put your lives at risk in unknown territory. Plus, wherever Lulu's mother is in the Twilight Zone, we won't know what we will encounter along the way. You two should stay put where it's safer."

Jasper thought that was fair enough, but Jayjay was disappointed, and so was Lulu.

But, Charlie, you could take them back to where they belong! Orla spoke.

But how would I know, though? I don't want to put them in danger. I still believe it's best for them to stay here.

Orla sighed, *if you say so.*

Thanks for understanding, Orla.

"Let us take you to the other side of the reef now that we know why you're here."

I smiled gratefully at him. "Thank you, Jasper."

He nodded back.

"Well? What are we waiting for? We'll be right behind you!" Sandy replied.

"Follow us!" Jasper said as he and Jayjay began to lead us to the other side of the reef.

It took a bit of a while to reach the other side of the reef. When we did reach where the coral ended, we were met with deeper, darker waters, smaller rocks, and sand dunes.

Then I felt Jasper put his hand on mine and I

looked at him.

"Hey Mindatar, I have been thinking because I know you said 'no' to us coming with you, but I believe we should come because like you said, 'you won't know what you would encounter.' Let us come with you; we won't just protect only you and Lulu, but your friends as well from danger that may lurk ahead of you."

He's right! He and Jayjay are offering a helping hand to you. That is also why you should let them join you! Orla said in my head.

"What about your reef?" I asked.

"Our reef will be okay. The creatures will miss us, by noticing what is happening right now," he replied as he looked at the creatures that must've followed us, worried about him and Jayjay. Jasper's cheek fins pulsed electrical waves repeatedly, sensing their feelings. He then slipped his hand out of mine and approached the worried fish as Jayjay followed behind him.

"Are you leaving us, Whisperer?" the fish asked.

He briefly nodded. "Don't worry, we will return home, I promise. I may not know for how long, but I know that we will one day. We will never leave all of you behind because this is our home, and we will stick to it just like coral."

That cheered the fish up. Then the front fish swam to Jasper's lips and pressed its head onto them as Jasper planted a gentle kiss.

Lulu witnessed what just happened and asked me, "Japper kiss fiss?"

"He did, Lulu," I said.

"Why?"

"There's a meaning when you kiss a fish; it means good luck."

"How do you know this stuff, Charlie?" Sandy asked curiously.

"The fishermen from Pollen Village told me," I answered.

"True, they know a lot about the sea and myths," Sandy replied.

"They do, Sandy, they really do."

When Jasper and Jayjay came back to us after saying their goodbyes to the fish, we moved closer to the unknown that stretched before us.

Seeing this new territory, a nervous feeling built inside my stomach. I guaranteed that Atom and Sandy were nervous, too.

When I looked at Lulu, her eyes were almost wider than her head, and her mouth was slightly open, as if it was the first time she had seen the other side of the reef. I slowly brought her close to my chest, and she said to me, "Pear told me 'bout the other side."

"Has she, Lulu? That tentacled freak who messed with my friends. She messes with them; she messes with me," I scoffed, thinking of her.

I wasn't happy when Pearl used Sandy and Atom to threaten Jasper and Jayjay. No one dares mess with my friends. However, Jasper and Jayjay, for now, I'd call them mates, not exactly friends just yet.

Jasper overheard and replied, "Let's not think about her. From now on, let's focus on getting that little, delicate fish home."

I agreed. Then I said truthfully, "I'm so nervous."

He understood. "I see your colours, Charlie, it's okay. We'll be here, and so will your buddies."

I smiled at him for being inclusive of my friends. Then I felt something gripping onto my arm. I looked and saw that it was Atom.

"Do you mind if I hitch a ride on you?" he asked.

I nodded. "Yes, dude. That's fine. You can ride on my back."

He smiled back. "Thank you." Then he swam onto my back. "Onwards, we go into the unknown!"

Sandy and I laughed, and I could hear Orla chuckling softly from inside my head. "That's the spirit, Atom!" I said.

"Let's go to...where do we need to go again?" Sandy asked.

"Orla's Deep Spirit Tree, deep in the Twilight Zone," I answered.

Hearing that, everyone was curious.

"A Deep Spirit Tree? That sounds interesting," Atom replied.

"I am looking forward to discovering that. What could possibly happen along the way?" Sandy said.

"Possibilities are limitless!" I said. "Let's start this journey!"

We began swimming into the new and dark terrain to start the journey of returning Lulu to where she belongs.

We wouldn't know what places or creatures we would encounter. But what could possibly happen when we make our way through the uncharted waters of Hybrainia?

There was only one way to find out.

Chapter 8

The reef was now far from us, and all around were sand dunes, huge pointy rocks with very little seagrass, algae and small, scattered, luminous corals. What made me very curious were these massive, colourful crystal pillars that formed on top of a long and huge hill stretching around and even away from us, glowing vibrantly with colours in the darkness. A few of the pointed rocks around us were covered in them too!

Here and there were schools of big fish that all looked like crescent moons with crystal formations on their bodies, swimming in the darkness. Some other smaller schools looked as though lanterns were hanging beneath them, glowing a warm orangey-yellow light as smaller starfish-like creatures hung onto them.

Seeing all these weird creatures, Atom let go of my back and swam near the fish. "Snap," he said.

He was taking pictures.

Every time he does, even when using an actual camera, he says that if he successfully captures a shot of something.

He then approached the nearby rocks that were covered in crystals and took pictures as well.

"Snap," he said again.

Lulu was watching him, and she asked me, "Why he saying that?"

"He's taking pictures of this mysterious place so he can study it," I said.

"What that mean?"

"It means to learn about something while observing it."

"Oh."

"Well, Atom can't take pictures of everything here; he might attract unwanted attention," Sandy said.

But then all the fish around us shushed us loudly.

We all froze in confusion.

No one spoke until Atom said, "Are you seeing all this?"

A nearby fish with hanging lanterns swam above him, and a starfish-like creature hopped off and landed on his mouth, shushing him up.

Everything was silent except for quiet bubbling.

Then, another fish with lanterns approached us and the starfish whispered in unison, "You will wake up Xanaarhaah."

"Who's Xanaarhaah?" I whispered back, curious. Why was it a long name for a creature?

The starfish pointed to a giant rock on our right, covered in sand and coral; it looked like it was a closed eye. We heard loud and monstrous breathing.

Our eyes widened as fear struck us at seeing how huge the closed eye was, realising that this Xanaarhaah was massive! Why did it even sound like an ancient name?

I turned to the starfish again and moved my hand across my pursed mouth as if I was zipping it closed and nodded.

We heard Atom struggling to pull the starfish off of his mouth. "Get... off... my... face!"

"Atom, stay quiet!" I whispered.

But he wasn't listening to me.

Finally, the starfish lost its grip on Atom's mouth but stuck to his hands. When he moved his hands apart, the starfish stretched with them. That ticked him off, and he yelled at the top of his lungs.

A shock ran down my body, and I quickly placed my hand over his mouth. His cry echoed in the water.

The closed eye suddenly opened, and it was glowing sky blue; the inner iris was green, and the pupil constricted.

We yelped in fear, and my friends quickly came and hid behind me. The creature rose from the ground and towered over us. The sand fell off the creature, revealing blue, red, green and dark-blue striped scales on its long, serpent-like body and little arms. The hill range with the crystals around us was the creature's body, and it all rose from the ground.

The starfish on Atom's hands let go and sank into the sand to hide.

"That's on you, Atom, you idiot!" Sandy exclaimed angrily. She slapped Atom, and his head spun.

"My bad!" Atom stammered. He stopped his spinning head with his hands.

"Who has disturbed my slumber?" the giant serpent's voice boomed.

A Giant Crystal Serpent? He is so much bigger in your eyes.

Why do you sound so calm, Orla? That is a giant, freaking, sea serpent that's about to eat us…or try to kill us in any way!

"We are so, so sorry we disturbed your sleep!" Jayjay yelled to the sea serpent.

It looked down when it heard Jayjay's voice and saw us. "**Reef creatures? My! I don't see that every day in my Crystal Dunes.**"

"Crystal Dunes?" I murmured under my breath.

It is the biome you are in; he protects it with his long body as the crystal-barrier hill range that you've seen. The fish see him as a protector of these dunes, Orla explained.

Right, I thought.

The giant serpent moved its head down to us. I quickly reacted and dashed in front of the serpent. "Stay back, Crystal Serpent! I'm armed!" I yelled as I swiped my hand to activate its blade form.

But there was a moment of awkward silence.

I looked at my hand, but it was still three webbed fingers. I quickly brought it back to my chest, closing my fist, and then shot it out again. That time, it changed into its blade form. "I really need to remember that!" I said under my breath. Then I pointed it at the serpent again and yelled, "Stay back, giant serpent! I have a blade, and I'm not afraid to use it!"

But the giant serpent showed no fear. Instead, he slowly placed his big clawed finger onto my hand and moved it down.

"*Cease your wrath, little one, for I, Xanaarhaah, the Crystal Serpent of these dunes, harm no one here. I protect every soul within and eat the ones that harm them. You look not to be threats and aren't from here*," the Giant Crystal Serpent said.

A feeling inside me knew the serpent was right. I moved my bladed hand down and narrowed my eyes. "I'm sorry for how I reacted, Xanaarhaah."

Xanaarhaah gently placed his clawed finger under my chin and moved my head back up so I was looking at him.

"*Apologise not, little Goddess, a misunderstanding like this is forgiven. In truth, I am satisfied to see you here in my dunes! For that, I am blessed, and I willingly bless you back with my welcoming, respect and my prayer, mighty Goddess of Hybrainia*."

I smiled at him, glad that we were forgiven. "Thank you, Xanaarhaah. But I need to tell you that we are here for a reason."

"*And what that may be?*" he asked.

"*We are trying to return this tiny and shiny fish to where she belongs, to Orla!*" Sandy shouted to him.

Xanaarhaah's eyes locked onto Lulu's bright light. He moved his head down to my friends as curiosity grew. "*'Orla,' you say, little Batfish? So unfortunate she lost one of her young! You poor, tiny and fragile future generation of the Deep Spirit Tree*."

Lulu was terrified by the giant beast that she hid behind Atom, and Atom looked horrified by what he was seeing as his drone pupils shook.

Jayjay curled her blue-tipped tentacles and brought them close to her cheeks. "Oh, you little poor thing! A tiny fish who is a future generation of the Deep Spirit Tree and Orla!"

From hearing Jayjay's tone and choice of words, I became a little confused, as if she didn't know about Orla.

They must've been in the reef for so long that they forgot their origins, Orla reckoned.

I mean… you did say that they weren't supposed to be in the reef and were meant to be…wherever you know.

Mersinganoid Cove and the Gloom Forest.

I creased my eyebrows as I went into deeper thought about those two interesting biomes, starting with Mersinganoid Cove.

Was that where Mersinganoids lived?

I remember Orla mentioned the tradition that she does with them. Is the Gloom Forest similar, or don't they do it because they're wild specimens? But from now on, I have had to focus on our task, which was getting Lulu home to Orla.

I came back down to my friends and Lulu squeezed herself out of Jayjay's tentacles and swam into my hands immediately.

"*From my understanding, you must be headed for the Twilight Zone?*"

We all nodded, except Lulu and Atom, because he couldn't understand what Xanaarhaah was saying, and Lulu was too frightened to nod.

"Yes, we are trying to get her home, and it's not

going to be a simple task when it's further from here," I replied.

"*Then I can help you*," Xanaarhaah suggested.

"Wait! Actually?" Sandy asked, flabbergasted.

"*Yes. But I can't take you all the way to the Twilight Zone because I can't go too far from my dunes. But I can take you to a place I know that's on the other side of here*."

We were all very grateful that Xanaarhaah could help us.

"That will be very lovely of you, Xanaarhaah. Thank you!" I said.

"Oh, thank you, Hybrainia!" Sandy exclaimed.

"Thank you, Crystal Serpent!" Jasper said.

Then, without wasting time, Xanaarhaah dug his snout into the sand and said, "*Hop on!*"

Jasper, Jayjay, and Sandy swam above his snout and onto the crystal formations further up his head.

Still confused as to what was going on, Atom looked at me and asked, "Why are they getting on that serpent thing?"

"He's going to help take us to a place that he knows is past his dunes. It'll be okay. Just hang onto me."

Atom went behind me and gripped on to my back again as I placed my other hand over Lulu. Then I joined the others on Xanaarhaah's head and rested on the crystal formations as Atom got off and rested beside me.

Xanaarhaah began to rise from the sand and lifted his long body up within the surrounding water. "*Hold on tight, little ones*," he told us.

We gripped onto the crystals and his tough scales. "Got that checked out, Xanaarhaah!" I said.

"*Very good*," he replied. Then he looked at the fish that watched us from below, and said to them, "*I must do these souls a favour. I will return to rest, my friends*."

The fish understood.

Finally, he began to swim in the direction we needed to go, making our way across the Crystal Dunes.

Xanaarhaah was definitely not lying about holding tight because he was moving *fast! Really fast!*

Luckily, after some time, we got used to the speed, and we were brave enough to take off one hand from his crystal-formed head and scales.

Jasper, Jayjay and Sandy were looking down at the passing crystals and glowing fish either resting or swimming around.

Atom was humming a song, Lulu was asleep in my hand, and I was just silent, thinking about the things that Orla mentioned earlier. The curious thoughts of mine refused to shake off, and that was okay.

Orla must've understood that she asked me,

Curious about those things I mentioned?

Yeah, I am. Can I ask you a question?

Anything you may ask me, Charlie.

What is the tradition of you and Mersinganoids, and why do you do it?

The Mersinganoids gather around a cenote in their cove, waiting patiently for my arrival. When I come to them, they give me treasures, like pearls and even the lost scales from their loved ones. After that, they will sing to me and my young until the Silver Moon rises from the horizon, signalling me to return home with the treasures the people had given me. It is a three-year tradition to them; they see me as a legend who will forever continue the tradition as long as I have all of my young with me to continue it. Lulu is extremely special and important for the next tradition because she is the newborn of my family.

And what do they do to the newborn?

They hold it in their hands, and their hearts will glow, feeling that special blessing as it flows through them like an ocean's current. They pass it on to each other, one by one, until it is eventually given back to me.

What's the purpose of that?

When they hold the newborn, that special feeling flows through them, making them happy that the newborn light is shared equally with them. In return, the Mersinganoids give it love and their welcoming to not just their home but also to all of Hybrainia's ocean, as it is part of a new generation.

Why do they give you their treasures like pearls and their scales? Are they for you?

The reason why they give me their treasures is because it's a gift for the souls of their loved ones that I would take to my Deep Spirit Tree.

I briefly nodded. *That makes sense.*

Then Orla said to me, *When you soon reach the biome Xanaarhaah is taking you, may I ask you a favour?*

Certainly! What do you want me to do, Orla?

Because Lulu can't hear me yet, may you teach her to use her telepathy?

I was a little hesitant, but I responded truthfully, *Umm… I can try if you give me a few tips.*

What do you mean?

I mean, like, tell me ways to help teach her to use her telepathy with me. It makes me think, if she figures out how to, does that create a connection so she can hear you and me together?

Yes, that is right. We have the ability to create connections to communicate with each other from living beings such as you, Jasper or any of your friends.

Cool! Yes, I'll try to teach her if you tell me some ways to help her.

It is not just with Lulu, however. If you press your head on any of your friends, I will create a telepathic connection with them, allowing me to speak to you and them either at the same time or privately to one in the connection. It is like creating a web.

Could that even work on Atom's drone?

Hmmmm… I am uncertain.

That's fair.

"What's on your mind, Charlie?" Atom asked me.

I jumped in surprise and looked at him.

My jump woke Lulu up.

"Speaking to Orla, that's all," I said. Then I looked at Lulu. "Your mum wants me to teach you how to use a super-power that you share with her, so you can communicate with us by using your mind."

Lulu softly gasped. "Really? A supa powa?"

I nodded. "Yes! But that is going to need a lot of practice, but I will help you. Maybe once we reach the biome that Xanaarhaah is taking us to. If you practice enough, you may hear your mum for the first time ever!"

Lulu's eyes sparkled, and her breathing quickened excitedly.

"**Maybe for now, you little souls should rest until we get there**," Xanaarhaah replied, overhearing our conversation.

I thought that was a good idea: none of us got sleep tonight because we were on the move, and it was dark. Our joints would be pretty sore from moving them for hours in the dark.

"What did it say?" Atom asked me.

"He said that we should rest. Same for you, Lulu."

Lulu nodded, then snuggled herself in my hand and went back to sleep.

"I'll hold onto your drone, buddy, while you get to the Den and join the others," I insisted to Atom.

He smiled softly at me. "Thank you. I'll reoperate this drone in the morning."

I chuckled. "Goodnight, Atom."

"Sweet dreams, Alpha," he said back as he snuggled into my arm so that I wouldn't lose him.

"Thanks, dude," I said.

He closed his eyes and shut down his systems for the night.

I closed my eyes too and went to sleep.

Sleep well, Charlie. Let your dreams loose inside of you.

Chapter 9

A mangrove forest, but underwater with giant mushrooms

Daylight finally arrived and we all slept during Xanaarhaah's journey of taking us to where we needed to go.

I had a dream that there were these humongous, glooming purple mushrooms with long roots stretching from the ground, holding the mushrooms up and in the surrounding waters. They looked as though they were hot air balloons but connected to the seabed with their roots twirling and pointing to the surface of the ocean. They were flesh, squishy and hollow on the inside with a hole in the bottom.

The sea creatures in my dream were unusual, too. They looked like giant pink and coquelicot-splattered sea slugs that were as long and large as dolphins with wings of a manta ray, covered in thousands of yellow and orange-tipped polyps on their backs, almost looking like fur.

Their nature was like bees: they were swimming to each of the giant mushrooms, rubbing their backs on them to collect some sort of aquatic dust that stuck to their polyps before taking it back to a colony in the centre of the giant mushrooms.

From my imagination, the biome looked like a mangrove forest, but deep underneath the water, the mangrove trees were giant mushrooms.

As I dreamed, I was exploring this mysterious place, unseen by those sea slugs, and I heard a voice whispering to me to find their queen and that she would help me with where to go next in the hope of returning Lulu to Orla.

But before I could keep exploring this mysterious place, I felt something tapping my chest gently, and my dream faded.

I opened my eyes and was greeted by Lulu's bright light, so I furiously closed them again.

"Gah! Darn it!" I exclaimed.

"Huh?" Lulu said, tilting her confused little round body.

I blinked rapidly until my eyes adjusted to her light. "Don't worry about that; it's something I just say for no reason."

"Oh," she replied.

Rise and shine, Charlie. Did you have a good dream? Orla asked in my mind.

I did, Orla! I had a crazy dream that there were these massive mangrove-like mushrooms and sea slugs pollinating them, like the bees on the mainland!

My, my, Charlie, that is a vivid dream!

"Slept well, Mindatar?" Xanaarhaah asked.

"Yeah, I did. I had a crazy dream that I was in this biome full of mushrooms that looked like mangroves, twisty roots that pointed to the surface, and sea slugs that pollinated them. My dreams are very interesting."

Xanaarhaah chuckled. "*My, what a coincidence. That is the place where I'm taking you, called the Mushgroves*."

I tilted my head. "Mushgroves?"

"*Yes. It is a very purple place where Mushroom Dust Sea Slugs pollinate the mushrooms to take the dusty stuff back to their colony for food. They all share the same scent to recognise one another as their workers or soldiers. The soldiers' scent is a little stronger than the workers'. They guard the outside for intruders, even if it wasn't their kind*."

"So if we had their scent, would they let us in?" I asked.

"*Yes, they would*."

"And if we don't?" Jasper asked, coming from behind me.

Me and Lulu got a fright that we both yelped.

Jasper jumped with surprise when he heard us. "Oh! Sorry, I didn't mean to scare you."

"It's okay, Jasper. You even scared Lulu."

"Sorry, Lulu," he said.

Lulu smiled at him and accepted his apology.

Then I felt Atom turning back on in my arm. "Good! Everything's working! What did I miss?" he asked.

"*Then they won't let you in*," Xanaarhaah answered.

Me and Jasper understood.

I moved Lulu off my chest to look at her for a moment as she stared back at me with a cute, friendly smile.

Maybe if we show Lulu to them, I hope that would explain enough as to why they should let us in when we get to the Mushgroves.

You could try, but see what happens. I believe you would be let in, no matter what, but you'll have to find a way to get your friends in, too, if they were denied.

I'll think of something, Orla.

Good on you.

"If my friends were denied access to the Mushgroves, I'll find a way for them to be granted access," I said.

Jasper smiled at me. "Thanks, Charlie."

I nodded. "No worries."

"Grant us access for what?" Atom asked, confused as to what we were talking about.

I explained, "We are headed for a place called the Mushgroves. There are Mushroom Dust Sea Slugs that will be guarding the outer parts of the place. I'll find a way to let you in."

He understood by nodding. Then he looked down and murmured under his breath, "Mushroom Dust Sea Slugs? Sounds like something for me to study!"

"*We're here!*" Xanaarhaah shouted loudly.

Sandy and Jayjay were woken by his loud cry and quickly came to investigate as we gazed at what was ahead, and all gasped.

There were purple mushrooms with twisty and looping roots that pointed to the surface, and they held the base of the mushrooms' caps in the water! A few sea slugs could be seen rubbing themselves against them and swimming further into the biome.

"Holy moly! What an ecosystem!" Atom exclaimed.

"That must be the Mushgroves!" Jasper said.

"It's very purple!" Jayjay added.

"That place looks alien to me," Sandy replied.

"*This was exactly in my dream!*" I exclaimed.

Everyone looked at me.

"Actually? How?" Sandy asked.

"I should be asking myself the same question!" I answered.

"Woooooow! Pwetty!" Lulu said, leaning over my hand.

"**You better hold onto something**," Xanaarhaah suggested.

I gripped his scales with one hand and held Lulu in the other while Sandy grabbed Atom. She and everyone else swam to a crystal or antenna to hold on, and Xanaarhaah began to dive down towards the place.

It took a bit of time to reach the ground, but eventually we made it. Xanaarhaah lowered his head to the ground, and we got off before he rose back up again.

"Thank you for your help, Xanaarhaah!" I shouted up to him.

"**Well it is the best that I can do to get you here. Continue your mission and bring her back to where she belongs. I wish you good luck.**"

"We will! Have a safe travel home, Xanaarhaah!" I waved at him.

Lulu waved with me. "Bye bye!"

He nodded before turning around and swam away, disappearing through the blurry distance of the ocean.

We then turned around and were greeted by the giant mushrooms ahead of us, standing tall and looking healthy as some Mushroom Dust Sea Slugs pollinated them.

At the entrance, it was guarded by two bigger Mushroom Dust Sea Slugs with three sharp-tipped tentacles that stretched from their backs and their patterns were splatters of coquelicot and magenta.

We approached them directly, and I went in front.

The guards lowered their heads toward me, and one of them said to me, "Mindatar? What a delight to see you for the first time! We are now blessed. We may smell your scent before letting you in."

Then two big suckers from behind their heads emerged and started sucking around me, smelling my scent. It really tickled me that I couldn't stop laughing.

After smelling me, they moved out of the way for me to enter. But first, I pointed to my friends, and said to the guards, "I appreciate you granting me access into your home, but may you grant access to them as well? There is a reason why."

"And why must we, Mindatar?" one of them asked curiously, looking at them.

I showed Lulu to them. "It's because we are trying to get this little Golden Starpearl home, back to Orla, and we need to speak to your queen for shortcuts or anything that could help us. If you can help us, that would be great."

"I want to go home," Lulu pleaded with dilated

white pupils, begging for them to let them in.

The guards looked at each other, then at my friends, who were hoping for a positive answer, and they thought about it.

After a moment, their eyes met mine again and they said, "Then let's make a deal, Goddess of Hybrainia. We can lend our scent to you, but promise that they won't hurt anyone, touch anything valuable, or bring a predator into our territory."

Jasper, Sandy and Jayjay nodded. Even though Atom couldn't understand a word they were saying, Sandy placed her hand on his head and made him nod.

I moved my hand over my chest and made a cross. "I cross my heart. It means that we promise."

The guards were interested. "Such a weird way of speaking, but we are grateful that you promised. If you wanna see our queen, then we will first spread our scent to you, and just follow this path. It'll take you straight to her. Your skin colours may change because of our slime."

"Is it permanent?" Sandy asked.

They shook their heads. "No, Batfish. Our slime and scent that we will put on you will wear off after some time, and you will go back to your original colours."

Sandy sighed with relief. "Oh good. I was worried that I would be a different colour for the rest of my life because I struggle seeing colours correctly."

Jasper looked at her. "Do you?"

Atom and Sandy both nodded at him, and Atom answered, "She has tritanopia colour blindness."

I gave the guards a kind nod. "We accept your offering of your scent to us!"

"Anything for you, Mindatar. Just hold still."

They swam closer to me, and I covered Lulu in my hands and closed my eyes and mouth when their bodies wrapped around me, and I felt slime being secreted all over me.

The movement of the guards gently rubbing me was very smooth but also very weird, especially with the slime being put on me. I barely opened my eyes and began to notice myself changing colour. The blue on me was turning into indigo, and the rest of the colours were red, pink, and purple.

Eventually, the guards moved away from me, and I smelled like salty honey. I was in different colours! Lulu stayed the same, however, because I kept her under my hands, away from the slime.

The guards went to each of my friends next, sharing their scent with them one at a time until they smelled just like them. After they unravelled from each of my friends, they were in different colours.

Sandy was indigo and purple. Jasper was a mix of dark and normal purple. Jayjay was still pink, but her jelly cap was purple, and so were her blue-tipped tentacles. Atom's white head and arms were pink, the red hydrogen behind his head had hot pink splatters, his blue chest was purple, his yellow belly was orange, and his legs were greyish-pink.

Once we all had the scent and our bodies had changed colours, the guards swam back to their positions and gestured for us with their tails to enter their territory, and we did.

As we passed them, Lulu peeked out of my hands again and waved at them with a huge, adorable grin on her face. "Bye bye!"

The guards gave her a nod.

I chuckled at Lulu warmly. "You're really cute, Lulu."

"Thank you, Charwie."

"You're welcome."

Suddenly, my stomach started growling, demanding input.

Everyone else heard my grumbling and looked at me.

"You're hungry," Atom said.

"Ehhh… I'm fine."

"I'm kinda hungry myself, actually," Sandy replied.

Lulu got a bit worried and she started shaking in my hands.

"No, Lulu. We're not going to eat you," I said.

Lulu sighed with relief. Then her tiny tummy growled.

"You must be hungry too, huh?" I asked.

She opened her mouth and pointed her fin at it.

I nodded, understanding. "I'll take that as a 'yes'."

Then, from a nearby mushroom, a female Mushroom Dust Sea Slug that was mindfully pollinating it overheard us and came straight to us. Her splatters were more vibrant red and hot pink. Her polyps were orange, and her antennas stretched past her head. Her eyes were on each side of her head, and her pupils were orange.

She circled around us, huddling us together and she asked, "On empty stomachs?"

We nodded.

Atom couldn't understand what she said, so he just nodded with us.

"Here, you can suck the honey off my polyps. Hopefully, that will fill you up."

She faced her back to us, which was full of the mushroom dust on her polyps and a sort of enzyme secreted onto them, mixing with the dust and turning it into a goopy, sticky slime.

From seeing that full process, Sandy thought it was so disgusting that she gagged. "I think I'm gonna hurl."

"What did I just witness?" Atom asked, not knowing what was going on.

I shuddered uncomfortably. Then I shook my head at the Mushroom Dust Sea Slug and answered honestly, "Thank you, but no thank you."

She spun back around and faced me again, surprised. "No? This is the only source of food we have. But what if you critters try our crystallised honey in our nest? Our queen wouldn't mind if you had some."

"Crystallised honey?" Jasper asked curiously, "That doesn't sound bad. What does it taste like? Is it salty? Sweet? Crunchy?"

"Our honey tastes very sweet and crunchy when crystallised. Our queen savours our food, too, to turn it back into liquid in order to feed the young that rest in her chamber. I can take you to her if you want."

My eyebrows raised, and I willingly nodded. "We actually need to see your queen because we need your help with directions to return this little Golden Starpearl home. I believe that your queen would have any ideas?" I showed Lulu to her, and she moved her head down to have a closer look.

After a few seconds, her eyes met mine again and replied with a warm smile, "Well, you came to the right place. How did you get here? I'm curious."

"Xanaarhaah. He's a Giant Crystal Serpent. He's such a kind soul of a protector he is of his dunes," Jayjay answered.

"Oh, Xanaarhaah! The neighbour who protects his Crystal Dunes. He's a friend of our queen, too. Such a great favour from him to bring you to the right place where our queen can help you. I will certainly take you to her. However, I don't think I can fit all of you onto my back, but I think I can fit maybe three of you," she said as she spun her body, facing us with her back again as her tail lay on the seabed. "Goddess and anyone else?" she insisted.

Me and Lulu looked at each other, and I shrugged. Then we both went onto her back, ignoring the feeling of the slime on her polyps.

Atom joined in next with me and Lulu.

Jasper insisted that Jayjay climb on, and she gracefully went on with us as he and Sandy stayed off. He turned to Sandy and insisted that she join as well, but Sandy shook her head and she waved her hands. "No thanks, I have speed. I prefer to swim than ride on her goopy back. No offence, by the way."

"Understandable," she said, "by the way, you can call me Lyly."

Lulu sounded amazed when the creature introduced herself to us. "I'm Lulu!"

"Lulu? That's a pretty name for a tiny future generation of the Deep Spirit Tree. You are a beautiful miracle, Lulu, especially to your mother."

Lulu didn't know what that meant, but she knew it was a good thing.

Finally, Lyly took us through the Mushgroves while Sandy and Jasper followed behind. As we made our way through, we looked around, amazed by the new environment we were in.

The giant balloon-like mushrooms towered over us and could even be seen from further away in the distance. Other Mushroom Dust Sea Slugs mindfully pollinated the mushrooms and took the dust they gathered in the same direction Lyly was taking us. Honeycomb-like coral clusters stood under the giant mushrooms we passed as small—perhaps juvenile—Mushroom Dust Sea Slugs peeked out and watched us from in bushy-looking red and pink sea shrubs.

Atom was taking pictures of the environment to study later after he logged off his drone body.

I looked at him. "It's really cool here, isn't it, dude?"

He nodded. "This place is fascinating. It honestly feels like we're in a different dimension."

"I hear you."

I took a deep breath, held it for a second, and let it out.

Jasper heard me and approached me. "What's on your mind, Charlie?" he asked.

I yelped with a surprised jump, causing Lulu to

nearly fall out of my hands. I looked left and right for Jasper until I turned my body to him, who was swimming by Lyly's right side, where I was sitting.

"Nothing. Just enjoying the view as we make our way to the queen. There's so much more than I thought there was underwater," I answered.

"Honestly, I never knew that the ocean was very vast either. I always thought my reef was the only place there was because it was on the edge of sand dunes. But now that we are past that, I've learned that there's more than just my reef."

"I was studying you last night," Atom joined our conversation. "I learned that Mersinganoids are social and usually in families, just like our people. You also sing a lot, either to attract the attention of a soulmate or just to interact and enjoy other peoples company. You, however, are very…unlike your kind. You must've lived in the reef your whole life, so that your memory was still developing, meaning you couldn't remember where you originally were."

Hearing all that come out of his mouth, Jasper's cheek fins slowly went down, and his eyebrows dropped in a frown. "What? What are you talking about? The reef is my home, and it forever will be."

Jayjay agreed and added, "We live in the reef with the fish and corals."

But Atom remained silent and stared at her. "Um…pardon me?"

Jayjay became worried and thought she had said something that offended him. "Are you okay, creature? Was it something I said?"

Atom remained silent, still confused.

I forgot he couldn't understand certain sea creatures such as Jayjay, but we could understand each other no matter what because most of us were naturally aquatic who spoke English and Hybrainian.

Jasper repeated what she said to him, and then he understood. Then he asked Atom, "How do you hear my best friend?"

"All I could hear was clicking."

"Clicking? You hear sea creatures differently?"

Atom nodded.

Suddenly, my stomach growled loudly again. Everyone, including Lyly, looked at me. My face turned pink, and I chuckled nervously as I placed one hand on my hungry belly.

"Are you sure you don't want to try my honey?" Lyly asked.

I shook my head at her. "No thanks, I'm good."

"Well, don't worry. We are almost to the nest; it's right ahead of us."

We all looked and saw this massive spherical nest that stood above the ground with long and thick roots. The Mushroom Dust Sea Slugs entered and exited what seemed to be holes that were everywhere in the nest. In the middle was a bigger hole where a pink, warm glow was emitting from within, and the entrance had orange crystals formed around it.

I was puzzled by seeing the outside of the nest as it was pulsing in some parts, and it was shifting colours of pink, orange, purple and red all around. *Orla? Is it just me, or is that nest alive?*

I sighed with relief. *Well, that's good to hear.*

We entered through the pink-light-emitting hole, and there she was: the queen of all Mushroom Dust Sea Slugs.

She was four times bigger than Lyly; her back and some other parts of her body were covered in crystallised honey. She was slightly transparent so that you could see purple eggs inside her belly developing. Around the ceiling were clusters of what looked like sacs of purple eggs. She looked similar to Lyly, but just slightly fatter and longer, almost circling around the chamber, leaving only the entrance we just went through.

"My queen!" Lyly said.

"Hello, Lyly. What have you brought here today?" the queen asked.

We got off Lyly and slowly approached the queen.

She was fascinated to see us, but definitely happy to see me that she gasped, "Mindatar of Hybrainia! What a delight to see you for the first time!"

She scooped me up with her tail and pressed my body onto her soft and squishy skin. Lulu was still in my hands and she was getting squished; she was grunting and straining, trying to get out.

I struggled to move my hand and pushed the queen's tail away from us. "I do appreciate the welcoming hug, but please be careful."

"Oh, sorry, Mindatar. What brings you critters and Mersinganoid here?" she asked curiously.

Lyly swam near me and answered, "Xanaarhaah brought them here, and they need your help, my queen. They are headed for the Twilight Zone because they need to return one of the Mother of Gold's babies back to her."

I showed Lulu to the queen and she looked. After a second, she moved her tail from under me to cover her mouth. "How unfortunate! A special little runt, separated from her family. Your mother must be worried sick about you."

Lulu nodded as gold liquid formed in her eyes. "I wanna go home."

"We know, Lulu, but we *will* get you home, I promise," I replied as I gently wiped the blobs off her eyes, and they solidified in my hand. Then, I faced the queen again. "Do you have any ideas on how to get us to the Twilight Zone?"

She pondered.

As she did, my stomach growled once again, and she heard it.

"You sound hungry. Here, you can have some crystallised honey from me. Lyly, do the honours?"

Lyly nodded. "Yes, my queen."

She swam to her back and started breaking off some crystallised honey using her flexible tail. When she thought she had enough, she came back and gave us each a shard of honey to eat.

I was a bit curious, and so were Lulu, Jasper, Jayjay and Atom—even though he couldn't eat with his drone body. So he stored it in his chest cavity.

I moved my piece around my hands as Lulu watched me. I smelled it and licked it to see what it tasted like. The surface felt like rough glass on my tongue, and the flavour was like salty caramel mixed with honey. I took a gentle bite and munched it with my teeth.

"This isn't bad," I said.

Lyly and the queen both smiled. "We are grateful."

Lulu licked it, too, and must've really enjoyed it so much that she continuously licked the surface.

Jasper and Jayjay both took a bite from theirs, and they enjoyed the taste that they nibbled on theirs happily.

Sandy was a bit hesitant about her piece.

Jasper looked at her. "Have you tried it, Sandy? It's pretty good."

"No, I haven't yet. A feeling in my gut is just saying not to eat it. I'm sometimes very picky," she said truthfully.

"I can sense that. Just take a small bite and let it process on your taste buds."

Sandy took a moment to think about it, then she brought the piece closer to her mouth and bit a small chunk off. She munched and let the taste process on her tongue. After a few seconds, she nibbled on the chunk.

Jasper must've known that she liked it, so he

smiled at her.

After our bellies were full of crystallised honey, we felt much better.

"Thank you for letting us have something to eat, your highness. It was really tasty honey that you have," I said.

Jasper, Jayjay, Lulu, and Sandy agreed with me.

"**My pleasure, little ones**," the queen replied, happy that we liked the honey. Then she continued, "**I do know a way to get you critters to the Twilight Zone, where the Mother of Gold will be grateful when you return the Golden Starpearl back to her. You must seek our related cousins: the Manta Ray Sea Slugs**."

A sense of surprise hit me because I remembered they were Orla's travelling servants! She said they travel far after sensing a dead corpse and bring it all the way to her!

"Manta Ray Sea Slugs. Got it!" I replied.

"Question is…where do we find them? *How* do we find them?" Sandy asked, swimming next to me.

"**It's no swimming in the shallows; you must go deeper under the waves to find your path. But be careful; there are monsters that will seek any light as prey as you venture beyond here**," she told us.

"Understood, Your Highness," Jasper replied, nodding.

Jayjay nodded with him.

I wondered if the Manta Ray Sea Slugs would take us to Orla.

They will agree to help. But be careful. Like the

queen said, 'it's no swimming in the shallows.' The deeper you go, the less light there will be, the more predators will be drawn to all of you.

We always will, Orla. Danger is no match for us as long as we stick and work together!

You have very great enthusiasm I have noticed, Charlie.

I am a great Alpha of my team, Orla. I'm always ready for anything, and no one gets left behind…ever!

That is good.

I smiled at Orla's response.

Then I felt Jasper's hands on my shoulders, and I looked at him.

"Why are you being silent? Is something wrong?" he asked.

Lyly was confused about my behaviour, too. "You have been silent. Is there something in your mind that you can't seem to just shake off?"

"**It isn't anything like that, Lyly. I know why she is being silent**," the queen answered.

We all looked at her.

"**The Mother of Gold is speaking to her. She knows you are all on your way**."

Lulu and Jayjay's eyes sparkled in amazement.

"She already knows we're on our way? How? That sounds magical," Jayjay said.

I chuckled. "It's called telepathy. She uses it to communicate with me, and soon you guys, too, when we get a chance You have that too, Lulu. I just have to teach you how to use it."

Lulu's eyes sparkled even more. "I…have it?"

"Yes. But it's going to require some time and practice until you can use it."

She nodded excitedly.

"I mean, me and Atom here already knew about this, and that is why we're here seeking help that you offered about the Manta Ray Sea Slugs. What even are they?" Sandy asked curiously.

"They are our related cousins who collect a corpse of any creature who died and was left behind to decay, so their souls are brought to her to live for eternity. She protects not only her young but also the Deep Spirit Tree and the souls with it."

"How do we find the Manta Ray Sea Slugs?" Sandy asked again.

"The Manta Ray Sea Slugs produce a glowing and sparkly blue trail behind them as they swim from place to place until they reach her in the deep. They would also create blue-glowing currents in the Deep Blue, where turtles pass them to get to their feeding grounds, where jellyfish are found. If you see the turtles, follow them until they take you to the currents."

"Where do we find the turtles?" I asked.

"You must reach the other side of the Mushgroves; just keep swimming forward until you see glowing yellow algae and smooth, rocky patterned hills all over the place in tall, wavy grass. Lyly will help take you to the other side of here. Be careful not to startle the turtles, though you may not see them at first. But find them quickly; their feeding time is close."

We nodded.

"Always careful we are, Your Highness. We'll keep a look out for the things you said!" Sandy replied.

"**Good. I wish you good luck in returning the Golden Starpearl back to the Mother of Gold. Lyly? May you take them to the other side?**" she asked her.

Lyly nodded. "Yes, my queen. Hop on, Goddess and Lulu." She turned around until her back was facing us.

We hopped onto her back.

She swam towards my friends and insisted that two more of them hop on. Jayjay hopped on, and then did Jasper that time.

Still having enough space for one more, I gestured for Atom to sit on my lap, and when he did, I wrapped my arm over him, securing him in place.

"It will be a little while before I get to the other side of my home; are you capable of waiting?" Lyly asked us.

We nodded.

We said goodbye to the queen and she shot a confident smile at us. Finally, Lyly took us out of the Hive Coral and in the direction of where we needed to go next, as Sandy followed close behind.

Lulu and I watched the giant Hive Coral as it went further away from us, and then we watched the other Mushroom Dust Sea Slugs doing their jobs.

As we did, Atom said, "Snap."

We all looked at him.

"It's for science," he replied.

I nodded.

"Who is Science?" Jasper asked curiously.

"Science is not a living thing; it is something that helps me learn about the world Charlie has created for us," he answered.

Jasper's cheek fins slowly lifted, and so did his eyebrows, amazed. "Tell me more!"

"How about when we get to the next place I have no idea where?" Atom said.

"The queen said we must keep a look out for turtles; they are the key to finding glowing blue currents that come from Manta Ray Sea Slugs, and *they* are the key to getting to Orla. But stay cautious because the deeper we go, the less light there will be and the more predators that lurk in the darkness, waiting to strike at us," I said.

Everyone nodded except for Lulu, who was terrified to the point that she was shaking in my hand. "Pwedatos! Hungry like Pearl."

I looked at her. "It's okay, Lulu. We don't have to worry about that, yet. As long as you are with us, everything will be okay. We will protect you, I promise."

Lulu smiled at me and then rubbed herself on my hand as if she was cuddling me. "Thank you, Charwie."

I lightly smiled as Lulu's affection touched my heart.

She's bonding to you as a best friend. She really trusts you, Orla said in my mind.

I can't say how much my heart is being touched right now.

That was also what the Mersinganoids did in the tradition. Even before something is born, love grows greatly in the heart and is given like an early gift.

Just like Bucky did to me.

"Charlie? Are you okay? I'm sensing you are really happy and sad at the same time," Jasper said.

"I'm okay, Jasper."

Chapter 10

A luscious grassland

As we neared our next destination, the giant mushrooms began to shrink down, followed by their roots that were buried under the sand.

Clicks and squeals were heard all around us, as if the ocean was singing to us, and the water around us turned light blue.

On the sand were small stalks of green beginning to sprout out and become longer, and we noticed small clusters of glowing yellow algae on them, just like the queen said to look for.

Just when we reached the longest of the grass, Lyly stopped, and we hopped off. I let go of Atom while I kept Lulu close to my chest.

"This is as far as I can go. Remember what my queen said and find the turtles and glowing blue currents!"

We nodded.

Sandy made Atom nod even though he couldn't understand what Lyly was saying.

"We will! We will find the turtles and follow them to the glowing blue currents!" I replied.

"I wish you good luck, and be careful of predators

that lay ahead!" Lyly added.

Jasper nodded briefly. "We will!"

"Very good. I must return home now and keep doing my duty for my queen. Stay safe!" She turned around and made her way back home as we waved at her.

"Say 'bye-bye,' Lulu!" I said.

"'Bye-bye, Lulu!'"

After Lyly disappeared out of sight, we all turned around to see this new place!

The ground was covered in seagrass! Very few fish and sea creatures, like dolphins with yellow on their heads, their two dorsal fins and tails. What amazed me was that a new species of Gippyguppy was here too, except they were mostly green and grey!

Their appearances were different. Their two axolotl-like antennae were longer than their eyes and more flexible. Their tails were the same, and they had different patterns on their bodies, too!

The green Gippyguppies had vertical wavy stripes to camouflage in the long seagrass.

The grey Gippyguppies had charcoal-like patterns to camouflage on the smooth and round patterned rocky hills and hexagonal formations that were nearby.

Speaking of those hexagonal formations, they towered so high they even stuck out from the water's surface high above us!

"This place is beautiful! It kind of looks like the Kelp Forest, but deeper, there's no kelp anywhere, and there is a new rock formation I've never seen!" Sandy exclaimed.

"This rock formation is called columnar jointing. This formation is made when igneous rock cools down, causing it to fracture into hexagonal shapes. Sometimes, when enough material is erupted, these formations protrude from the water and create an island!"

I was mind-blown by how Atom knew all of that!

It's impressive how he knows this! Orla replied in my head.

"How do you know all of this, Atom?" Sandy asked.

Atom chuckled. "I studied geology!"

I looked around this beautiful place, my eyes sparkling as much as Lulu's.

Then, I thought that this place was good to start teaching Lulu about her powers.

Wise choice of yours, Charlie, Orla said, knowing what I was thinking.

Thank you. Now, what are the most important powers that Lulu needs to learn?

Telepathy. In order to do that, she has to focus her mind on a soul in order to independently create a telepathic connection, as I did with you. We will start hearing her voice in your head if she focuses hard enough.

I nodded. *Got it.*

I released Lulu and she swam toward the seagrass to check it out. As her light touched it, the seagrass grew longer and longer. She giggled as she watched it grow higher than her.

"Okay, Lulu," I said.

She turned to me.

"Your mum needs me to teach you how to use your powers. The first one you are going to practise is your telepathy."

"Telepappy!" she exclaimed excitedly.

"Yes. All you have to do is focus your mind on me as hard as you can. If you focus hard enough, you will start hearing my inner voice, and soon, your mum's voice too!"

Hearing that, Lulu clapped her fins excitedly and made happy noises. "Mama! Mama, hear me?"

"Yes! Mama will hear you if you focus hard enough! Now, let's do it, Lulu! Focus your mind on me. I believe in you!"

Lulu nodded. Then she closed her eyes and pressed her blue fins on her head to focus her telepathy on me.

C'mon, Lulu! You can do this! Hear my inner voice! Soon, we will hear yours too!

Lulu focused really hard until she started to glow brighter. The seagrass around her grew longer. But then she opened her eyes again and dropped her blue fins off her head, panting in exhaustion. She took a second to catch her breath from her first attempt, then looked at me with a frown.

"It's okay, Lulu, you don't always get it on the first try. But I believe in you. Don't be hard on yourself. Try again and keep concentrating!" I encouraged her.

Hearing those words come out of my mouth, her smile was restored, and she continued concentrating on her telepathy.

As she did, the others came and watched with

curiosity.

"What is she doing?" Atom asked.

"She's practising her telepathy; I know she can do it. I believe in her!" I replied.

Jasper grinned at me, and his eyes moved back to Lulu as she started getting as bright as she was on her first attempt.

Her light grew stronger, and it caught the sea creatures' attention around us as they approached, their curiosity growing also.

The green and grey Gippyguppies came close to Lulu as they watched, their pupils dilated.

The seagrass around Lulu grew longer, satisfying some of the Gippyguppies to the point that they began eating it.

Then, from a small glimpse, Lulu slightly opened her eyes, and her white pupils suddenly dilated so enormously that they almost covered her pink sclera! She stopped when that happened, shaking her head.

We saw what happened and were more curious as if that was supposed to happen.

"Lulu? Are you okay?" Jasper asked.

Lulu took a moment to find her words. "I saw…blackness and sparkles…looking like you!"

"You saw blackness and sparkles that looked like us?" Sandy asked.

She nodded.

Jayjay looked at me. "Why don't you ask Orla, Charlie?"

I nodded and did what Jayjay suggested. "Orla? Were Lulu's dilating pupils meant to happen?"

I nodded, understanding.

"What is she saying? Is it meant to happen?" Jasper asked.

I told my friends everything, and they understood.

We all faced Lulu again and encouraged her.

Seeing us encourage her, the Gippyguppies all looked at each other for a moment and decided to join us, and they cheered her on.

"You can do it!" one grey Gippyguppy said.

"We believe in you!" a green Gippyguppy shouted.

More and more of the Gippyguppies cheered her on!

Lulu looked around as they did, amazed that she couldn't help but grin excitedly. Then, for the third time, she concentrated on her telepathy again, harder than she had before.

The more she focused, the brighter she shone.

I cheered her on in my head. *C'mon, Lulu! A third time's a charm! We know you can do this! For your mother! You are almost there!*

Finally, Lulu's eyes widened, and her white pupils dilated so that they covered the pink in her eyes. Then a huge wave of light burst from her and into the surrounding ocean!

We had to quickly cover our eyes before we were blinded. But when it was gone, we were all okay. Amazed grins filled our faces and the Gippyguppies howled and cheered with pride!

"She did the thing! Now what?" Sandy asked.

Lulu looked at the Gippyguppies around her and finally at us. Her eyes were as bright as she originally was!

She finally did it! She learned her first power! Once she creates her telepathic connection to you, you will be able to hear her inside your head! Orla exclaimed happily.

I nodded, still smiling. Then I spoke with my inner voice, *Lulu?*

Lulu gasped.

I raised my eyebrows, wondering if she actually heard me. To prove that it was true, I asked Lulu with my thoughts, *can you hear me?*

Lulu's grin slowly came back, and she nodded quickly.

I...I can hear you! I can hear all of you at the same time, but you all are not moving your mouths!

You can hear all of us? I honestly didn't know you could talk clearly when you are using your telepathy!

Yes! It feels very strange! Mama? Can you hear me, Mama?

I could hear Orla gasping with delight as she was about to cry. *Oh, Lulu! I hear you! My little Golden Starpearl's first power!*

I love you, Mama!

I love you, too, Lulu!

Lulu swam to my Mindatar symbols, her eyes changing back to normal as she approached. She put her tiny fins on and pressed her head against them as if she were trying to cuddle Orla inside my head.

My friends swam around me and watched Lulu's cute behaviour.

Jasper was so touched that his chest started glowing, revealing the blurry figure of his beating heart inside.

Atom noticed and was so fascinated that he wanted to get a closer look, but then he suddenly stopped, and the red metal molecule-like bulbs behind his head started flashing and beeping.

The noise frightened the Gippyguppies, and the green ones hid in the seagrass while the grey ones fled to the basalt formations to hide.

We all looked at Atom.

"That's bad. Really bad! We need to find those turtles now!" he cried with fear.

I grabbed Lulu with one hand and quickly swam to Atom to calm him down. "Atom! Atom! Calm down, dude! What's wrong? Why are your metal hydrogens making an alarm noise?"

"Why did all the Gippyguppies leave because of your alarms?" Sandy asked, suspicious.

Jasper and Jayjay both looked around, feeling scared as if something was nearby.

Suddenly, a red tentacle appeared and separated me from Atom.

We all yelped with surprise!

I kept Lulu under my hand, and we all noticed a large gap on the seagrass below the tentacle. Then, five familiar glowing eyes appeared in front of me. A body then emerged from the thin water and towered over us with its five menacing eyes.

It was Pearl!

"*There you are!*" she snarled.

"That's impossible! I knocked you out cold! How did you find us?" I exclaimed.

Pearl chuckled sinisterly. "I wasn't actually unconscious, Charlie. It was a trick, and you were all dumb enough to fall for it. I followed you from the very start because you made me use my other trick: camouflage. I know what you are trying to do to my little snack." She moved closer to us.

Lulu was so terrified of Pearl that she couldn't stop shaking.

"You are trying to bring her to the depths of the sea. But I found her first, fair and square, so she belongs to me!"

She attempted to snatch Lulu out of my hand, but I quickly moved back.

Seeing my action, Pearl got so angry that she clenched her tentacle. "How…dare you! Give me the fish!"

She tried snatching Lulu again with more of her tentacles, but I quickly swam back to avoid her arms.

"No! We refuse to give Lulu to you! She doesn't belong to you, even if you found her first!" I yelled.

Pearl's face boiled, her pupils shrunk greatly and her breathing roughened. "You'll regret saying that in front of my face! Soon, you will be begging for mercy, and you *will* surrender the fish to me, you stubborn, little brat!"

I eyed Pearl intensely as she growled at me

But then Atom said, "Maybe before Pearl tries to eat all of us, we should swim for our lives and find those turtles!"

I quickly glanced at everyone before looking straight back at Pearl last as she brought up all her tentacles from the seagrass.

"Swim!" I shouted.

So, we did! I quickly swam under Pearl before she could catch me in her arms, and we all fled as she chased after us!

"Hide!" I cried as I dove under the seagrass.

The others did the same thing hiding under the long seagrass.

Our frantic movements disturbed the grass all around Pearl, confusing her as she tried to find me and Lulu. She separated parts of the seagrass to look for me and Lulu.

I did my best to cover as much of Lulu's light as I could, but the slightest rays that escaped through my hands touched the grass and made it grow longer.

Lulu was breathing rapidly, and I tried my best to calm her down by shushing her before Pearl could hear us.

I'm scared! What if my light gives us away? I don't want to be eaten!

Neither do I, Lulu. We will find the turtles before Pearl finds us!

What about the others? Will they find us too?

Yes, they will. We just need to escape Pearl and reunite when we can!

I hope Pearl doesn't find them and that they are alright!

I'll make sure that they will be alright as long as they stay under the seagrass!

I wasn't paying attention to where we were going in the seagrass, and I suddenly bumped into someone in front of me. I looked up and saw it was Jasper!

"Watch it!" Jasper exclaimed quietly, rubbing his head, not knowing it was me.

I sighed with relief. "Jasper!"

Jasper! It's you!

He looked up when he heard me and sighed with relief too. "Oh, Charlie! Lulu! You're okay! Where are the others?"

"I don't know, but I hope they are okay and hidden," I whispered.

Taking the risk, I quickly peeked my head out of the seagrass and saw Pearl looking around the other disturbed moving grass for my friends and even stabbing her tentacles to search for who was in there.

"*Where are you? Stop moving, and let me catch you!*" she yelled.

Worry filled me as I realised our friends were in danger!

I went back under the seagrass and whispered, "Pearl is targeting Atom, Sandy and Jayjay."

Jasper and Lulu gasped.

"We need to get them out of there! But how?"

Jasper whispered.

I had to hatch a plan in order to get Pearl away from them, and fast!

As I tried, Lulu started to cry golden tears again. Seeing this, Jasper tried to calm her down by gently shushing her.

When I saw the glowing tears, a clever idea popped into my head. "I have a plan. I'll use Lulu's tears to distract Pearl and lure her away. This will give you enough time to get them out of there. Keep Lulu with you, too, and make sure Pearl doesn't see you; I don't want to risk putting you in danger again. I'll catch up once I find a way to shake Pearl off me."

This could work! Pearl will be fooled! Orla said.

What about you? Lulu asked with her telepathy, worried.

"I'll be okay. Stay with Jasper, and he'll keep you hidden," I replied.

"I'll hide you in my mouth," Jasper insisted.

Lulu was frightened as she remembered what happened back in the Kelp Forest. I gave him a shocked expression.

"I let fish come into my mouth because they trust me. I never swallowed any of them. I know it's weird, but it will keep her hidden from Pearl's eyes. Trust me."

I thought he made a good point because I remembered he had done it to Lulu to get away from my friends, and he had taken me with him. So, I agreed.

I gave Lulu to him, and he scooped her up in his hands, leaving her tears behind for me to use, and gently shoved her into his mouth. As he moved his hands away and closed his mouth over her, Lulu's light could be seen shining through his dotted nose.

He then stuck out two fingers on both his hands and gently hit his fists on top of each other as he gave me a faithful look in his eyes.

I knew it was sign language, but I didn't know what he was saying.

He's saying 'be careful', Orla translated.

I gathered the golden tears that shone and floated in front of us and merged them to almost the size of Lulu. Then I rose out of the seagrass as Jasper stayed under, keeping Lulu safe and well hidden in his mouth.

I gazed at Pearl, who had now cornered them onto a columnar jointing formation and was ready to attack them!

I swam closer until I started hearing what Pearl was saying to them!

"I am giving you one last chance to tell me where she is! Tell me where she is!"

Sandy shook her head. *"We will never tell you!"*

Pearl grew so furious that she grabbed each of them in her tentacles tightly as she growled at them.

"Very well then! If you don't want to tell me, then I will have to find her myself! But first, I could use a little bite, starting with you three!" She opened her mouth, which was full of razor-sharp teeth!

Jayjay, Atom and Sandy all closed their eyes and turned their heads away as Pearl's teeth drew closer to them.

Anger filled me, and I shouted at Pearl. *"Hey,*

kraken head!”

Pearl heard me and stopped right when their heads nearly touched her black teeth. She lifted her teeth away from them and turned to me.

“*I command you to let them go!*” I yelled.

Hearing what came out of my mouth, Pearl laughed hysterically as she loosened her grip on my friends, but still held them. “Make me! I stand respectfully at the top of my food chain! Everyone should fear me, including you!”

“Even the biggest of apex predators in the sea? I am not afraid of you!”

Her laughter turned into a sinister chuckle. “Exactly what a coward would say. Now are you here to give me the fish?”

“As a matter of fact, you are right! She's right here!”

I opened up my hands, and the tear's light shone brightly, making Pearl believe it was actually Lulu. Her five eyes widened, and she let go of Atom, Sandy and Jayjay, who thought I was actually giving Lulu to Pearl, not knowing it was a trick.

Pearl began to approach me, but I swam back and shouted, “*But if you want her so badly, then come and get me, six-armed freak!*”

Pearl's face boiled red when I called her that, and she began to chase after me, leaving Sandy, Jayjay and Atom.

Be careful, and don't let her catch you! Orla exclaimed.

I quickly swam to the basalt rock formations, where the grey Gippyguppies hid, and went around them for as long as I could to buy Jasper time. I avoided Pearl's tentacles that attempted to catch me, even her ferocious snapping teeth when she got too close. Very few times, I nearly had my feet stabbed, but I didn't give in.

As the loops around the same formation became noticeable, Pearl suddenly stopped in place, and I was too slow to realise. She wrapped her tentacle around my foot, stopping me from continuing. She pulled me a little closer and reached another tentacle for my hands. "*Gotcha! Now hand it over!*"

"*In your dreams!*" I exclaimed, moving the light onto my belly as I quickly brought one of my fists up, swung it to change into its blade form and sliced through her tentacle that held my foot.

Pearl screamed in pain, and I resumed the chase.

I went for another formation that showed more of the smooth, large, patterned rock hills, and I noticed Jasper and the others sneaking under the grass to stay out of Pearl's sight.

When Sandy noticed me, I started hearing her voice from my amulet. "Charlie! Jasper told us your plan to buy us time! Do you see these hills? They aren't hills, but the turtles we are looking for! If you can keep Pearl distracted for long enough, the turtles will rise and start moving!"

I grinned and did everything I could to continue the chase!

But after a few seconds had passed, I began to feel the blob of tears beginning to solidify in my hands. I was alarmed and worried that if Pearl noticed, she would realise it was a trick.

No no no no! Just hang in there a little longer!

The tears are about to solidify! Hurry! Orla exclaimed.

I lost my attention to my surroundings and I noticed a great shadow towering over me. I looked up and saw a massive formation that protruded over the water, and I quickly slowed down until I came to a stop in front of the basalt.

A dead end! Come on turtles! Wake up already! I thought as my hand that held the solidifying tears hopped with them.

I turned around, and Pearl trapped me by stretching out her two longer tentacles around me. She grabbed me with two of her smaller ones, wrapping one around my waist and the other on my bladed hand.

I held the failing light under my normal hand. Luckily, Pearl didn't notice.

"I have you now, and there is nowhere else to swim! You were impressively swift, but it wasn't enough, Charlie. I finally caught up to you, and I knew I would get you! Now, for my prey!"

Pearl snatched the light out of my hand with another one of her small tentacles and she moved me closer to her menacing eyes. "You came so far, but you failed, Charlie! The hunter…always…wins!"

Before Pearl could do anything else to me, the ground began to shake. She looked around, confused as to what was going on.

I noticed behind her that the turtles slowly started getting up.

While Pearl was distracted by the movements, I quickly brought up my bladed hand that she was holding on to and bit her tentacle, making her scream. She turned back to me with glaring eyes and slammed me hard onto the basalt rock behind me.

"That's what you get for biting me! There's nothing you can do now that I have the fish!" she exclaimed.

Then from behind Pearl, Sandy came charging and impaled her spines on another one of Pearl's tentacles.

"*Leave our Alpha alone!*" she cried.

In more agony, Pearl tried to shake her off, and her spines slipped out.

Sandy quickly came to me and pulled me out of Pearl's weak grasp, and we both made a swim for it.

Pearl watched us as we hurriedly approached my friends, and we got on the nearest giant turtle. Her evil grin crept onto her face. "*Swim away, little fools. I now have the fish, and there is nothing you can do to stop me!*"

We all stared at her as the giant turtle we were on rose from the seagrass, ready for the big journey with the rest.

Pearl brought her closed tentacle, which she believed she was holding Lulu, and opened it, only to see a large golden pearl.

Her five eyes widened with shock, realising she had been tricked. "*Are you kidding me? A golden pearl? Where is she?*"

Jasper opened his mouth to reveal where Lulu was.

When Pearl saw Lulu's true light, she was so

enraged she threw the pearl onto the seagrass and slammed her tentacle hard onto the basalt behind her, causing it to crack and fracture, and she screamed.

"Get duped, idiot!" Sandy shouted as she laughed.

As the giant turtle we were on took us further and further away from the underwater grassland and Pearl, relief filled us, knowing we were safe…for now.

However, my back was in a lot of pain, and I was coughing, which made it harder to breathe.

Jasper let Lulu out of his mouth and he held her in his hands as all my friends came and checked on me, worried.

Sandy laid my head on her arm and held my hand with hers. "Charlie? Are you okay?"

I moved my weak gaze to her as I struggled to take deep breaths.

You're hurt! Lulu said with her telepathy.

She got you good, didn't she? Orla asked in my head.

I struggled to find my words.

Atom came closer and held my bladed hand. I closed it, and I felt it turn back to normal.

Atom asked Sandy to carefully lift me up to check my back for fractures, cuts or dislocations, and she did. When she raised me high enough, Atom let go of my hand and moved behind to check if I was alright.

I coughed again.

Then, very quickly, my lungs started to feel like they were being healed, and my back pain was relieved. I could breathe normally again, thanks to my regenerative power.

I heard Atom gasp. Sandy leaned in to see what was going on, and she gasped softly.

"Fascinating! You even share the symbolism of the Kyanite Wisp!"

I glanced at him, surprised. "And that is?"

Atom moved back into my vision. "Healing! They can heal other creatures much quicker than naturally! In your water form, you can heal any creatures *and* yourself!"

My eyes widened with surprise. "Why didn't I know that before?"

"Charlie? How are you feeling?" Jasper asked, gently holding my hand, which Atom once did, as he held Lulu in his other.

Lulu and Jayjay agreed with his question.

"Better than ever!" I answered.

Jasper smiled. "That's great to hear. I kept Lulu safe while you distracted Pearl."

He brought Lulu closer to me, and I reached my hands for her as she moved off his, and into mine. I brought her onto my chest as she stared at me with a huge happy smile on her face before cuddling me. *I'm so happy you're okay! I don't like it when I see you get hurt. I get scared.*

"Well, Lulu, risking your life is sometimes worth it for others. I'll do it for anyone, and I don't need anything in return." I slowly stroked her tiny head with my thumb. *But you didn't have to do it.*

"It was the only way to protect you guys. Where would you be without me?" I asked Lulu.

Everyone agreed.

Lulu took a moment to think. *I would be lost without any of you to help me get home. I would have been caught and eaten by Pearl.*

"Oh, sweetie," Jayjay replied, "you were lucky to find us to take you home. It's amazing that we have come this far already! Speaking of which, Charlie? Where do we need to go next?"

"We now need to keep a lookout for glowy and sparkly blue currents. I have no idea where they would carry us when we do find one in the Deep Blue. But who knows what could be on the other side of them? Hopefully the Manta Ray Sea Slugs the queen told us about," I replied.

Everyone nodded, hoping I was right.

I glanced at the passing basalt formations and seagrass behind me, even some Gippyguppies that watched us from within as we began to enter deeper waters. Then I looked up to see the surface, which I knew I wouldn't be able to see later until our mission was complete.

Finally, I looked ahead, took a deep breath and let it out slowly; bubbles escaped my lips. *Though you may still be far, Orla, there's more to learn about the ocean.*

You are right, my dear.

I wonder what it's like in the Deep Blue? Lulu wondered.

Only one way to find out, Lulu, I said in my head.

Chapter 11

The giant turtles finally left the underwater grassland after a bit of time, and the seabed gradually went down the deeper we entered.

All of us watched what was below as we passed several biomes. Atom captured photos of the exotic creatures and plant life down there for later study.

Because of the strong flow of water we were going against, the scent that the Mushroom Dust Sea Slugs gave us started to wear off. We all looked at our hands and watched them until it was completely gone, and our original colours had returned.

"Finally! I'm back to my normal colour! Am I back to my normal colour?" Sandy asked.

We nodded.

"Oh good!" she sighed.

"I have to say I missed being in my normal colours; it felt like I was going to be in different purple colours for longer," Jasper said.

"I was pink the whole time, except for my back fin, teal cap and tentacles, but now I'm happy my colours are back," Jayjay replied.

Lulu smiled widely. Then she yawned.

I looked at her as she snuggled in my hands and rested her eyes.

I yawned, too, and everyone heard me.

"Tired?" Jasper asked.

I nodded.

Jasper tilted his head and smirked softly. "Why don't you lie down and close your eyes?"

I shook my head. "I can't, Jasper. We need to keep a look out for the currents, and I'm too scared to miss them."

"Don't worry, Charlie, we'll keep our eyes peeled for them. When we do see them, I'll wake you up. You can rest on my lap."

Butterflies filled my stomach, and my face heated up. I covered my face with my arm and looked away while I held Lulu in my other hand. "Thanks, but I'm good."

Jasper crawled a little closer to me and gently moved my arm off my face. "I insist, even if you say no. No need to feel sheepish. I can hold Lulu for you, and maybe I'll sing for you both to sleep?"

I raised my eyebrow. "Are…are you sure you really want to do this?"

Jasper raised his shoulders softly and grinned. "Why wouldn't I be? I wish all living things in the sea to have a good slumber, you too, Charlie."

I thought about it for a moment. Finally, I nodded and gave Lulu to him. He let go of my arm and gently took her into his hands. He then crossed his legs and patted his lap for me.

I steadily shrunk my size until I was small enough to fit in his lap. I climbed in and laid myself on his right leg. I felt him lay his hand over me, covering my body and caressing my head with his thumb as he began to sing.

His gentle voice was so soothing that it was like a siren singing a lullaby of the sea to me. Even Jayjay and Sandy felt sleepy, and Atom was trying so hard to stay awake.

So…beautiful, I thought as I entered a deep sleep, thanks to Jasper's voice.

His voice began to fade away, and so did the water's ambience.

I began to hear different sounds around me, like the ethereal voices and whispers of singing ghosts, and the ambience was quieter, yet almost silent. I felt like I was drifting in the water and not the turtle I was on with the others.

There were bright lights from outside my eyelids, and a familiar voice started talking to me.

Rise and shine, Charlie.

But I just dozed off.

You have been asleep for thirty minutes.

Already? It feels like one minute.

It does feel that way when you sleep. But you are still sleeping, though you are dreaming of something you must see.

Something I must see? What is it, Orla?

Open your eyes.

I brought my hand up to rub my eyes, but suddenly, it felt like it was phasing through my face! I opened my eyes and pulled my hand off my face.

I looked at my hand and saw it was transparent. I moved my other hand, and it went through it.

How do I do that?

I quickly realised my lips weren't moving; that was definitely a sign I was in a dream, but what was the dream about? Orla said it was something that I must see. So, I looked up and in front of me was a giant, shining golden kraken with one eye, staring at me with two of its humongous tentacles spaced out between me.

I yelped in fright without moving my lips and tried to swim away backwards but hit an invisible barrier behind me. I turned around and placed my hands on the barrier.

What is this? Why can't I get out? Where am I?

You are in my Deep Spirit Tree, Charlie.

Hearing Orla's voice again, I turned back to the kraken. I noticed giant twisty and glowing golden-tipped branches around us, harbouring the souls of deceased creatures of many species, including the souls of Mersinganoids who hummed and harmonised with their songs.

My eyes sparkled in amazement at seeing this incredible place. The tree was full of ghosts and a golden light, the same as the kraken's.

Some of the souls were looking back at me, and some Mersinganoid ghosts even came up to me, placing their hands on the invisible barrier.

Most of them looked very old, while others were younger.

I slowly approached them and placed my hands where they touched theirs on the barrier. They smiled at me, and some of them passed their foreheads on it.

I felt their joy, and I smiled back.

I then looked at the kraken as it showed me a harmless expression in its giant eye, and I said, in my dream, *Orla?*

It is me, Charlie.

You're a kraken? You are huge!

To me, you are a tiny goddess of Hybrainia.

Fair. This place is beautiful!

Beautiful indeed, yet very ancient and full of souls that grow my tree.

No wonder why you call it the Deep Spirit Tree.

Orla chuckled, then carefully moved me away from the souls of the Mersinganoids so she could show me around the tree. I looked around with curiosity.

There were souls everywhere, big and small, scary and majestic!

They all watched me, shot their wide and friendly smiles, and waved. I waved back at them as Orla began to unwrap her tentacles from the branches to move off the centre, revealing a small nest beneath her. She brought me to the nest, and I saw tiny golden creatures that shone nearly as brightly as Lulu.

There was a prawn, a squid, an octopus, a crab, a sea angel, a koi, a guppy and an eel, all sleeping.

I thought there were only species like Lulu. I was wrong. But I soon realised that the babies weren't having such a calm slumber; I could hear their sorrowful cries.

They're worried about Lulu, aren't they, Orla?

She nodded. *They know how important and special Lulu is to them, and even when she was still in the egg, so did the spirits of my tree. Without her, we are incomplete and would fade in despair for our lost sister and daughter. That was why I called for you in your dream back on the surface when you were sitting under the lilac sky and that light that you saw under the water.*

Wait! How do you know that dream?

I made it so you could hear my desperation for a hero such as yourself. I knew you would respond to my distress.

A sudden realisation hit me in the chest when Orla told me that. *So not only are you telepathic, but also psychic!*

I am the creator of dreams in the sea, too. Those dreams you've been having were from me.

So you knew where to take us all along?

Not for all, for I don't know a lot about the unexplored shallower parts of the ocean. I'm too big, and we only come up to Mersinganoid Cove every three years in the summer.

Fair enough. I don't know much about the deep ocean either. But can you tell me where Mersinganoid Cove is and what it's like?

I can show you in your dreams.

How do you do that?

It's simple; all you have to do is close your eyes in your sleep, and I will make it show in your dreams. You won't see me anymore, however, but you will still hear me.

I nodded. Then I closed my eyes so Orla could work her magic to show me Mersinganoid Cove.

From outside my eyelids, I noticed the brightness changing around me, and the sounds of birds and swishing water were heard.

You can open your eyes now, Orla's voice whispered.

I did just that.

Around me were Violet Palm Trees and pointy shrubs where little bugs flashing blue lights were resting.

Under my webbed feet, because I was still in aquatic form even in my sleep, the ground felt moist and muddy because it was protected by the trees' shade, making my surroundings a little dark and mysterious.

A path awaited me ahead, so I followed it. As I did, I looked around, my curiosity getting the better of me until I stopped at a big, dark cave with webs that hung glowworms of so many colours. My eyes sparkled at seeing their beauty. But then I noticed, on the other side, a glimpse of a cenote and a few living Mersinganoids chilling on the rocks, singing their song.

Mersinganoids! They look like Jasper but in different colours and fins.

They are just like your people but connected to the sea, Orla replied.

Wanting to learn more about the special importance of Mersinganoid Cove, I entered through the sparkling cave and into the area, discovering the cenote was way bigger than I thought. All of the Mersinganoids that I could see were under the shade of the trees, while some others were under the water, swimming.

So, this is home to the Mersinganoids. I remember you saying that you come here every three years for a special tradition with them. What is it about?

The reason I come to them every three years is so that I collect the remains of their loved ones, listen to their songs and share their love with all of my young. It's a special tradition for the aquatic people.

How did this tradition come to be? What's the history behind it, Orla?

It all started when their ancestors explored the deepest section of the ocean, and they came across me when I and the Deep Spirit Tree were smaller and younger. They were amazed when they found me and thought I was the brightest thing that they'd ever seen, brighter than the sun itself. They gave me their own shared blessings and their cherished treasures before returning to the shallows. Three years later, they visited me again. They prayed, shared the love in their hearts with me and even sang to me. They saw me as a legend. The next three years came, and they returned to pray and share their love with me. By the time they were about to return home, I followed them, curious to find where they came from. After weeks of following through the distant underwater lands I never knew existed, I found where they came from.

So when they found you, they knew they could trust you.

I nodded, agreeing with Orla.

Then, I thought about Jasper and wondered what

he was doing right now. Would he also be asleep, or was he still keeping a lookout for the currents? As I did, my surroundings began to crumble and fade away, back to Orla and the Deep Spirit Tree.

She knew what I was thinking as she had read my mind. *Why don't you open your eyes and see if Jasper is still awake? If he is awake, I ask you to create a connection with him so I can talk to him.*

But how do I wake up?

Allow me. I am holding your subconscious, and if I close my tentacles over you, you will wake up from your sleep. This won't hurt, I promise.

I trust you.

Hearing that, Orla showed me a positive expression in her giant eye, and she closed me in her tentacles as everything began to fade into blackness.

Soon after that, I started hearing the sounds of the currents we were pushing against again.

I slowly adjusted my eyes. As I blinked to see properly, I found myself back on Jasper's lap with his hand still over me. He still held Lulu in the other hand near his chest.

When he noticed I was awake, he moved his hand off my body and gently lifted my head to help sit me up.

"You're awake. How did you sleep?" he asked.

I rubbed my eyes. "Interestingly."

I got off Jasper's lap and grew back to my normal size.

I saw Sandy, Jayjay and Atom had fallen asleep while gripping the turtle's shell to avoid being left behind.

Jasper tilted his head curiously. "What makes you say that?"

I explained Orla made the dreams I had previously, and she told me the history of the tradition of his kind and the bond they had made with her.

His eyes widened, and his cheek fins rose as electrical pulses went through. "There's actually more of me?" he asked.

I nodded. Then I added, "Orla has asked me to do a favour, and that's to get you part of the telepathic connection she has made with me."

"And how do you do that?"

"By pressing our foreheads together," I answered as I pointed my thumb to my forehead and my pinkie finger to his. After doing so, a funny feeling in my stomach began to fill, and I looked away.

But Jasper easily detected what I was feeling, and he smiled. "It's okay to feel nervous, Charlie. It's for Orla, isn't it?"

I nodded.

He moved closer to me as he held sleeping Lulu. His movement woke her up, and she yawned. She then watched to see what was going on.

"We're friends, and friends do favours for them, and I'm willing to do yours, Charlie. Let's start small."

Hearing those words come out of his mouth, I felt more comfortable, and I took deep breaths, bubbles escaping my lips. I said to myself, "Here it goes," and we pressed our foreheads together.

Jasper. If you can hear my voice speak to you, my name is Orla, and I have so much to tell you.

Jasper, can you hear me?

Jasper gasped.

Can he hear her? I thought.

Can you hear me in your mind, Jasper?

Jasper's breathing slightly quickened, and he said, flabbergasted, "I...I hear you, Orla! I hear you!"

He hears you, Mama! Lulu said with her telepathy; her breathing became excited.

We could tell that Orla was super happy. *That is good to hear!*

Joy hit my chest, and I started to laugh.

Jasper laughed with me.

Our laughter woke Sandy, Jayjay and Atom up with surprise and confusion.

"What? What's happening? Have we found the currents yet?" Sandy asked, her eyes drooping.

"What's so funny, Jasper and Charlie?" Jayjay asked with a yawn.

"Sorry for my absence; I must've dozed off to Jasper's singing," Atom said.

Charlie and Jasper made my mama's magical connection grow! Jasper can hear my mummy now!

Sandy and Jayjay's eyes widened when Lulu told them telepathically, and they smiled.

"How did you do it?" Jayjay asked Jasper.

Jasper used sign language to tell her what we did, and then she understood. Sandy didn't know what he was saying, but Atom did.

Suddenly, we heard Jayjay gasp at something and yell, "Look! It's the currents the queen told us to look

All of us except Atom looked, and she was right!

We saw strong currents ahead of us, and the turtles were approaching it!

"Atom, look!" Sandy pointed, and Atom turned his head to see. His mouth then dropped in amazement!

It's the currents! There are so many of them! Wonder which one it is! Lulu wondered.

"Look for blue sparkling light!" I said.

We kept our eyes peeled for one current with sparkling blue light; that was where we must go next in order to take another step closer to Orla.

As the turtles entered through the currents, we searched hard. Finally, my eyes caught some sparkling blue light in a current that was split below us, and the light was going to the left. I pointed and shouted, "Over there!"

They all turned and looked, and excitement filled them.

"Good eyes!" Jasper said.

I chuckled. "Now we just need to catch it and find the Manta Ray Sea Slugs!"

"But how? The turtles are only going through the currents! We're high from the one we need to go through!" Sandy replied.

She was right: the current we needed to catch was too far down. So we had to think of a way to get to it.

After a few seconds, Atom said, "I have an idea!"

We all looked at him.

"I noticed some of the currents are connected, so if we take this one up ahead of us, we can ride to the one down there! But we'll have to stay left to catch the blue current because if we don't, that other one will take us somewhere else, somewhere we don't want to be."

Atom pointed to the current that the turtle we were on was approaching, which was close enough for us to catch. We connected the dots and then nodded, believing Atom's idea could work.

"Good thinking, dude! Good thing you came along with us! We just have to time it right, and we will be in that flow of water in no time. It might get a little bumpy, so I hope you guys don't throw up!"

"We've had strong currents in the reef before, but this is nothing compared to ours!" Jayjay replied.

"Hey, guys? Sorry if I'm interrupting, but we've got unwanted company!" Sandy stammered as she pointed at something from behind.

We all looked and saw another creature latching on and moving from turtle to turtle, coming towards us.

Seeing who it was, shock rocked our spines.

It was Pearl again! Turned out she was not giving up that easily!

Lulu gasped and hid under Jasper's hands in fear.

"Oh, you have *got* to be kidding me!" I exclaimed.

"*Here? When? How? She doesn't even have suckers!*" Atom cried.

"You may have your ways, Atom, but she has hers too!" Jasper stammered, his cat eyes constricting and his scales on his shoulders and forearms flaring.

As Pearl came closer, latching on and off from turtle to turtle, she gave us a ferocious glare. "*Missed me?*" she shouted.

"*No!*" I shouted back.

"*Well, too bad! You thought you left me for good! But I'm not giving up that easily!*"

"*We can tell!*" Sandy shouted.

I turned around again and saw we were about to get near the current that would take us to the one we needed to go. "Okay! On three, we jump!"

Everyone faced my direction too, and waited for my cue to jump.

"One…" I started counting.

I glanced and noticed Pearl becoming larger the closer she came.

"Two…"

I felt Atom climbing onto my back; his breathing was rapid as if he was hyperventilating.

The current grew closer.

After a few more seconds, Pearl finally reached the turtle we were on. At that exact time, the current was only a few metres away from us.

"I have you now!" Pearl exclaimed as she licked her teeth.

Finally, I shouted, "*Jump!*"

We all jumped just before Pearl could grab our feet, and we went into the current that started taking us away from her and the turtle we were once on.

Pearl growled angrily at her failure and jumped off to follow us in the current.

The current took us down. Atom held onto me tightly as Jasper did for Lulu, hiding her in his hands.

Sandy tried her best to control herself by propelling against the flow with her aquatic wings, but Jayjay was screaming and waving her tentacles crazily.

Pearl struggled to control herself in the powerful flow of water as she tried to get to us.

As we began to near the sparkling current, I shouted to my friends, "*Move left!*"

We swam to the left-hand side of the current as fast as we could. It took us a bit of time to stay left, but we managed to hold on there until Pearl caught up to us and tried to grab us.

We managed to stay away until she caught Jasper's foot and tossed him to the opposite side of us, taking Lulu with him.

"*Jasper!*" we cried in horror.

We reached where the currents split, and Jasper and Lulu ended up in the wrong one.

Pearl went after them.

I quickly forced Atom off of me so I could go after him and Lulu. The others panicked at what I did as I entered the current Jasper and Lulu were forced into.

"*Charlie!*" Atom screamed.

"*No!*" Sandy cried.

"*We will find a way back to you!*" I shouted as the currents began to spread away from each other, separating us.

Then I turned to Pearl as she attempted to snatch Lulu out of Jasper's hands, and he did his best to shield her and get away. I dashed forward and pushed Pearl away from them. That angered her more, and she targeted me and tried to snap her razor-sharp teeth at me. I managed to avoid every bite she attempted and punched her face, causing her pain so that she covered the spot where it hurt, and I used my abilities to control the flow of water to throw her out of the current.

Once again, Pearl was gone for now, but we were going the wrong way, and the current was so strong that it was impossible to get out!

I noticed in the distance another current was connected to the sparkling current Sandy, Jayjay, and Atom were in, and they were pulled out of it, taking them in another direction.

As we were taken further away from Pearl and our friends, we struggled to control ourselves in the flow.

To keep Lulu more secure, Jasper quickly shoved her into his mouth again. Then he reached his hand out for me.

I struggled to reach him and even tried to get closer by kicking my webbed feet. After a few moments, we managed to touch the tips of our fingers and soon finally grabbed hold of each other. He pulled me to him, wrapping me around his arms and legs to secure me, and we closed our eyes, hoping we'd reach the end of where this unknown current was taking us.

Chapter 12

Lost in the Deep

The current took us deeper than we were before. Eventually, we ended up in a completely different biome.

This place was as dark as Xanaarhaah's dunes, but some mushrooms stretched high from the seabed. Their stems were a lot thinner than the Mushgroves', with a creamer colour, and the caps were flat, showing off mesmerising colours of green, yellow, pink, orange, and white. Not only were there mushrooms, but the terrain was mostly flat, as far as we could see from the bioluminescence they produced. The seabed was layered with a bluish-lavender, spongy, and squishy surface.

Unique, bioluminescent, red fan-like corals stuck to some non-spongy areas, and purple seagrass were under the tall mushrooms, along with smaller versions of themselves.

The current began to calm, but it brought us so low to the seafloor that we rolled on the spongy surface until it finally ceased.

Jasper let go of me and I slowly got up as he opened his mouth to let Lulu out. He then sat up.

My head was spinning so I placed my hand on it. "Beaver's dam. That was intense."

Are you three alright? Orla asked, worried.

"I…think so," I replied.

What happened? I'm scared! Lulu started breathing rapidly as she shed golden tears that floated into the water around us. I gestured for Lulu to come to me, and I gently held her in my hands as she cried. It took a moment for Lulu to calm down.

I raised my head to look at the water above us.

We were so far down because I couldn't see the surface or the sparkling current. It was also darker where we were as if we were more than a hundred metres down from the surface.

I began to feel a mixture of fear and worry building inside my body. "No…no, no, no, no, no! This can't be happening! There has to be a way back to them! There *has* to be!"

I looked around rapidly, my heart racing and my breathing quickened.

Lulu wriggled out of my hands and stared at me as I nearly had a panic attack.

I quickly pulled myself together. "It's fine! It's fine! Everything's going to be okay, Charlie! Just calm down and use your head! We *will* find a way back to them, right Jasper?"

I looked at Jasper, but I saw that he had tucked his knees and his arms wrapped around them, and he hid his face.

"Jasper? Are you okay?" I asked; my fear dropped, and my worry for him grew. I approached and went on my knees on the ground in front of him.

He looked at me, and I saw that his pupils had dilated. He trembled, "Do I look like I'm okay? This is all my fault! I should've given Lulu to you, and this wouldn't have happened because of me! This also feels…familiar. Have I been in those currents before? Was that how I was on the reef?"

His cheek fins dropped, and he hid his face under his arms again.

I took a second to search for my words.

It all makes sense as to how he was on the reef now.

What makes sense?

He was washed away from Mersinganoid Cove by the waves when he was little. The currents took him to the reef. I can see his early memories. Jayjay must've had the same thing as him. Can you look around again? This biome familiarises me.

I looked around again for Orla. After a moment, she gasped softly in realisation. *This is the Gloom Forest!*

So, we're in Jayjay's original biome?

I told you!

Probably, if Pearl hadn't forced us into that current, we would've been with the others and never found this place.

"Atom was right," I heard Jasper say, "maybe I wasn't supposed to be in the reef. But where am I supposed to be, then? I feel empty now. I feel like I lost everything on purpose. Now, I don't have a purpose. I don't know who I am anymore."

He began to sob.

Shock filled me, Lulu and Orla when he said that.

"Why are you being like this? You're Jasper, the Whisperer of the Reef! You look up to the reef and do everything you can to help. You promised them you would return home after all of this is complete," I said.

"What's the point if I never come back?"

"The creatures look up to you! You're their protector and best friend, and even more, you're like family to them! They all look up to you! Jayjay looks up to you! I look up to you!"

I placed my hand on his shoulder. "You're a very brave Mersinganoid! When I first met you, you were very mysterious. By seeing you again at the very start of this journey, I realised how kind and gentle you were to the smallest and most fragile of beings, like Lulu. You encouraged us and kept us together as a team! Where would we be without you?"

Jasper glanced at me for a moment, then asked, "Why are you trying to cheer me up?"

My heart sank a little bit, not feeling if I made him better. I don't like when people ask that in a depressed tone; it makes me feel a lot less confident in myself, too, because I sometimes think my comfort wasn't working. But it was still worth a try.

I slipped my hand off his shoulder and replied in a quiet, gloomy tone, "I do my best to make them feel better, just like my Alphanians would to me. I can't fix mistakes for others, but I try as much as I can to encourage them to keep going and never give up. Not only do I encourage *them*, but I also try to encourage myself, too, whenever I feel down. If that doesn't work,

I lowered my head to the ground as my confidence dropped, and I felt hopeless if I could ever return the favour.

I sighed.

I closed my eyes and rested my hands on my knees.

Then, I felt something touching my hands. I opened my eyes and saw Jasper's blue hand on mine. His other hand was on my chin, and he lifted my head so I could look at him.

Hearing what he said, I felt much better, and I smiled widely.

He smiled back and wrapped his arms around me, giving me a hug. I wrapped mine around him and gently squeezed him, happy that he was feeling better. Lulu joined in; she swam to the middle and placed her tiny fins on Jasper's cheek.

That is a good thing, Jasper. Even if it isn't your real home, you still see it as yours. You tend to keep it that way, and I'm okay with it.

"Thank you, Orla," Jasper said.

We let go of each other and went back to our feet. Jasper nodded at me, and I returned it, showing that my confidence had been restored. "Wonder where the current took the others?"

"Who knows? But there's only one way to find out," Jasper replied.

Maybe they will tell me with their inner voices! Lulu thought.

"We now have a team to reunite and a Golden Starpearl to return!" I said.

We then made our move through the Gloom Forest to start our new quest in mind: find our friends *and* return Lulu.

But we also needed to be careful as to what predators would be lurking in the darkness of the underwater mushroom forest and maybe hopefully find help.

Wherever the current took Sandy, Jayjay and Atom, we hoped they were alright and searching for us too.

Chapter 13

Higher up from Charlie, Jasper, and Lulu's location, Atom, Sandy and Jayjay roughly drifted in the wrong current. Their journey through the flow lasted a little longer.

Eventually, they ended up in another biome, which was much brighter than the one Charlie, Jasper, and Lulu were in.

The biome was similar to a Kelp Forest, but the seagrass was mixed with ferns and smaller kelp. Scattered within the area were spiky trees that looked like underwater yuccas.

In the surrounding water were floating small balloon-like plants that sprouted into small and large lily pads under the water. Small and colourful eels rested on them while some wandered everywhere. Other eels wrapped themselves around the ferns' leaves, moving with the flow of the gentle current.

Before Sandy, Jayjay, and Atom fell onto the ferns, the eels saw them just in time. They moved out of the way to avoid being crushed or stabbed by Sandy's spines.

Sandy was the first to be thrown out of the strong current, and she stopped herself by propelling her aquatic wings the opposite way. Jayjay and Atom were last, and they crashed into Sandy from behind.

"Watch the spines!" she exclaimed.

"Sorry!" Atom said, sucking his teeth, relieved he didn't get anywhere near her stabbing spines, or his drone would have been killed.

They looked around their new area, confused and lost.

"Where are we? Where's Charlie, Jasper and Lulu?" Sandy asked.

"I...don't know. I don't even know where Jasper and Charlie are. I hope they're alright," Atom said.

"Me too," Sandy replied.

But a few seconds later, Jayjay started to sob. Sandy picked up on her distress and immediately came to comfort her.

Atom, unfortunately, couldn't understand her emotion.

"Hey, hey, Jayjay. Don't cry; everything's going to be okay," Sandy said softly to her.

She can cry? Atom thought with surprise.

Jayjay glanced at her and trembled, "How will everything be okay? My best friend is gone! Charlie and Lulu are gone! I don't know what to do!"

Sandy grabbed her blue-tipped tentacles and her. "Jayjay, look at me. We might be lost, but I have a great sense of smell and hindsight! I can smell anyone from kilometres away!"

Jayjay's eyes widened upon hearing that. "You...you can?"

Sandy nodded and started sniffing the water in an

attempt to find Charlie or Jasper's scent. She sniffed the water for a few minutes. Because of how long it took, Jayjay started to lose her confidence if Sandy didn't pick up their scent.

Eventually, Sandy stopped smelling the water and looked at Jayjay and Atom with disappointment. "Nope. Got nothing."

"So much for 'kilometres'," Atom quoted.

"Shut up! I'm trying! If you say it was 'so much for kilometres,' then what's your plan?"

"It will be impossible for you to pick up their scent unless we had something that came from them," he answered.

Sandy placed her hands on her hips and gave him a glare. "Oh yeah? Like what, genius?"

Atom pressed the button on his blue drone chest, and it opened up, revealing a scale inside. It followed along with the crystallised honey he had stored earlier back in the Mushgroves. He took out the scale and showed it to Sandy. "We'd be *truly* lost without this!"

"A scale?" Sandy asked, puzzled.

Jayjay gasped and approached Atom with relief and excitement. "Not just any scale, Sandy, that's Jasper's scale! How did you get it?"

Atom just looked at her, showing a blank face.

Jayjay remembered that he couldn't understand her. "Oh, I forgot. You can't understand me."

Sandy soon realised Atom was right. "You're right! We'd be truly lost without that scale! Also, Jayjay is asking how you got it."

"When we were making our way to the left of the

current before we got separated by Pearl, Jasper lost one of his shoulder scales, which I learned acted like armour. I managed to catch it and keep it in my chest cavity."

Hearing that, Sandy was mind-blown. "You are a freaking genius!"

He chuckled as he closed his chest cavity and passed the scale to Sandy. "When in doubt, smell it out, Sandy Swaan."

Sandy retrieved the scale from Atom and brought it close to her gills between her eyes.

"Batfish senses don't fail me now," she said to herself. Then she took a big sniff of the scale and let her senses process the information they had been given. From her eyes, she started to see a path that led behind to her left. She pointed in the direction and shouted, "They're this way!"

Jayjay giggled happily as she followed behind Sandy.

"Right behind you, Sandy…literally," Atom replied as he grabbed Sandy's spine nearly at the back of her head.

"Yeah, yeah, I get it. Let's go! We've got a team to reunite!"

They made their move through the biome in search of their friends by using the scale that came from Jasper. They were super lucky they had that scale; otherwise, they would have truly been lost.

"You're really lucky I came along," Sandy added.

"As a matter of fact, we are," Atom replied.

Chapter 14

Not alone

Me, Jasper and Lulu made our way through the Gloom Forest, wary of any movement that could be from nearby predators lurking in the darkness. Mostly, it seemed peaceful, but we kept our guard up just in case.

We passed each tall, flat-capped mushroom, or Gloomshrooms which Orla told us what they were. Sometimes, adult Jelly-Capped Squids were seen munching on the caps, as on the underside were transparent egg sacs with embryos of developing baby Jelly-Capped Squids inside them. Seeing a few of the babies break free from their egg sacs was adorable.

"Seeing those baby creatures reminds me of when I first met Jayjay," Jasper said, smiling warmly.

"Does it? How come?" I asked.

"When I first met her, she was as small as them and very fragile. She was also a very scared little thing, but I showed her that peace was in me. I told her a little bit about myself, my name, and then we became best friends."

I smiled. "That's good you became best friends. How old were you back then when you met her?"

"I…don't remember, but I only know that I was

smaller."

"That's fair enough. When I bloomed into our world, I still remember most of the things I experienced, like taking my first steps, discovering my first creatures and making my very first friend, and I find him…very handsome."

I blushed and chuckled as I thought about Chuckboi.

Jasper smiled, sensing what I was feeling.

Orla already knew by reading my mind. *It's that red reptile you have a crush on.*

Jasper must've heard her in his mind because he showed a surprised look. "You like someone?"

I nodded. "He's something you've never seen before; you might have, back in the Oceanic Mountainside, but maybe just barely. He's what we call a Dragadillo. He's like an armoured dragon with a long tail and magical eyes that allow you to easily pick up on what he feels. He's very loyal and has a big heart."

"How did you two first meet?" Jasper asked curiously.

"We first met when we were younger and I was as tiny as a mouse. I used to be cared for by spiders, but they all feared him and believed he was dangerous because he ate them. One of the spiders jumped onto his shoulder and stabbed their fang through his tough scales, injecting venom into his bloodstream. The spider then tried to escape, but it had to rip off that fang that got stuck in his scales, leaving behind the attached gland. Because of it, it was poisoning him near extinction. I had to save him. So, as brave as I was, I climbed onto his shoulder and pulled it out as hard as I could. However, after succeeding in getting that fang out, one of the spiders got so angry that they wanted to bite me next. But then, instead of running away from all the spiders and me, he took me with him. After days passed, we learned about each other and realised we weren't so different, either from just species."

"What made you two so similar?"

"He's the last of his kind, and I'm the only Mindatar in this world. I promised him that I would protect him from the far future that may try to hurt him, and he does the same for me, even though I'm immortal. We've been together for so many years. He truly adores me and I truly adore him. We always have each other's backs."

His smile grew warmer. "Sounds like me and Jayjay: we always have each other's backs."

"That's what a well-developed friendship is. When you have people by your side, anything is possible."

Jasper agreed.

As we made our way through the biome, I decided to check on Lulu and see if she could still hear Sandy and Jayjay. "Do you hear Sandy and Jayjay?"

She looked at me with a frown and used her telepathy to talk to me. *I can't hear them!*

My eyes widened, worried. "Why not?"

I...don't know. I can't hear their voices!

Me and Jasper's eyes moved up to our foreheads as we heard Orla speak. *Her telepathy can't reach out from afar yet like I can, meaning she will lose the connection with Sandy and Jayjay unless she's close enough to them.*

Right…well, that's bad! I thought.

My eyes met Lulu's again and I said, "We'll have to find them sooner! But we can't rush through here, as we don't know what's lurking in the darkness."

Jasper agreed.

It's true, my Golden Starpearl. Just stay close to them and you will be safe.

Lulu's worry was replaced with confusion when Orla called her by what she was. *I'm not Golden Starpearl, I'm Lulu. You named me, Mama.*

You are right that I named you, but I call you my Golden Starpearl for a special reason, little twilight.

You call me Golden Starpearl for a reason? What do you mean, Mama?

"Orla already told me the reason why she called you that," I said.

Lulu's eyes widened. *She did? Why did you call me Golden Starpearl, Mama?*

Because, my beautiful little baby, you shine like gold, you are as bright as a star and as small as a pearl. That's why I called you that. Jasper's kind called me the Mother of Gold, because I am as golden as you. But you and your brothers and sisters shine brighter than me.

Her surprise turned to amazement. *I have brothers and sisters? Do they look like me?*

Not exactly like you. You were the last one to hatch; that was after we accidentally lost you in a storm. But you are in good hands, my dear, and as soon as you know it, you will see me for the first

Lulu smiled and clapped her fins as she giggled.

Jasper and I smiled at her cute expression.

But then, we heard the sound of distant whale song higher above us. We looked up and saw huge black figures that looked like whales with blue glowing dots on their bellies, slowly swimming in our direction.

"Wow! Dark small creatures! Where are they going?" Lulu said, verbally this time.

"They don't look small," Jasper added.

"They look like whales, but with blue luminescent spots under their chins and around their bellies."

That is a pod of Blue-Spotted Whales. They always travel to the south to feed in the Summertime. They would sometimes pass above me. Maybe if you follow the whales, they could lead you to me! Orla said.

"But what about Sandy, Jayjay and Atom?" I asked.

The pods are scattered across Hybrainia's seas. They all go to the same place, even passing where your friends may be!

Jasper and I looked at each other, a mixture of hope and worry at the same time.

"I hope Sandy, Jayjay and Atom know what they are doing," I said.

He agreed.

Suddenly, from further behind us, we heard a loud echoing grunt of something familiar landing on the spongy surface. We turned around and gasped in fear as we noticed five glowing yellow eyes in the distance, slowly shifting to orange around its eyes.

The creature huffed and puffed roughly and shouted, "*You thought you left me for good? You thought I was no longer after you? No! No, no, no, no! You only made me angrier. I was going easy on you at the very start, Charlie! But I won't anymore if you keep refusing to give…me…the…fish!*"

Pearl was back! She grabbed the stem of a nearby Gloomshroom and ripped it off the ground with rage. With another, she bit off the top half of it, which floated in the water as she spat out the torn stem from her mouth. She then scanned the area for us.

"*Where are you?*" she snarled.

We quickly looked for a place to hide before Pearl spotted us. The area around us as we swam through the mushrooms started to become hillier, hopefully increasing the chance of finding a cave.

Luckily, we managed to find one because of the blue, glowing aquatic vines that hung from the mouth of a cave nearby, and we went inside to hide.

As Pearl's growling gradually grew louder, Jasper hid Lulu in his mouth again and I held my breath to stay silent, hoping that we wouldn't be spotted. When it felt like Pearl was right at the cave where the vines hung, I closed my eyes and prayed. *Please don't come in. Please don't come in. Please don't come in!*

Just be silent and don't move, Orla said in our heads.

We waited as Pearl's rough growling started to fade until we couldn't hear her anymore. Taking the risk, I peeked to check if the coast was clear.

Pearl was nowhere to be seen.

I turned to Jasper and whispered, "Coast is clear."

Jasper nodded, then moved his hands in front of me to use sign language, but I couldn't understand what he was saying.

He's saying he wants to keep Lulu in his mouth to keep you hidden. He didn't realise that Pearl had become so much more vicious than he last saw her, Orla translated.

"No joke. Also, good thinking. Now come on, let's follow those whales and find our friends before Pearl *finds us*," I replied softly.

Jasper nodded again. Then we carefully went out of the cave, moving the glowing blue vines aside, and looked up to see if the whales were still there. They were, and we made our way through the biome, seeking safety in the darkness and behind rocks for as long as we could.

However, as we progressed, I started getting worried that my bioluminescent patterns all over my legs and arms could give our position away. The only lights Jasper had were his eyes, cheek fins, and flippers, which meant he was less bright than me.

To be more safe than sorry, I shrunk myself to the size of a mouse, swam onto his left shoulder, and held onto his scales as he swam.

He must've felt my presence and glanced at me, confused. He quickly swam to a large rock to hide in case Pearl was around, then gently moved me off his shoulder so I was in front of him.

To try and communicate, despite Lulu in his mouth, he pointed at me for a second, then placed the tip of his fingers onto the right side of his forehead and spun his index fingers.

He's asking if you know sign language.

Hearing what Orla told me, I shook my head at Jasper.

Don't worry, Jasper. I will translate what you say to her.

He was relieved when Orla told him in our minds. So, he continued using sign language to communicate with me.

He is now asking what is wrong and why you are so tiny.

I made a gesture to show him how glowy I was in my appearance.

Orla easily read what I was thinking. *You are worried that your glowing appearance could give you away, and you are trying to hide yourself.*

Jasper must've heard what Orla said as he continued using sign language.

He's saying that he doesn't think he can fit you and Lulu together in his mouth. So he's insisting that you stay close to his shoulder for as long as you can.

I nodded as he moved me back onto his shoulder. Then we kept going by hiding behind the rocks he could find to stay out of sight.

We continued until the seabed below us began rising upward, and the Gloomshrooms began to shrink, giving us a sign we had left the biome. Where we had now entered was another sand dune; this time, it was flatter, with no crystals, and it was devoid of life.

We looked up again and saw the whales were further ahead than they were before. We had to hurry and catch up to them. Before we entered the dunes, we looked back to make sure Pearl wasn't around. We did see her, but she wasn't facing in our direction and was still searching every single bit she came across, from lifting big rocks to moving the vines inside caves away.

We left the rocks we once took as hiding spots and escaped into the dunes.

When we were far enough out of Pearl's peripheral vision, he let Lulu out of his mouth, and I hopped off his shoulder to return to my normal size.

"That was close," I said, sighing with relief.

"For now," Jasper added.

"Pearl just refuses to give up that easily; she is a lot more determined and…what should I say…aggressive!"

"No kidding. I have never seen her like this before, and it scares me," he said as he shuddered, the scales on his shoulders and forearms flaring.

"Same here. C'mon, let's follow those whales and find our friends."

"Good idea."

We made our way through the dunes as Lulu stayed close to Jasper.

We didn't know where the whales would take us or what places we would pass through, but they were now our new guide to not only get to the Deep Spirit Tree but also to reunite with our friends at some point.

"I hope Sandy, Atom, and Jayjay find us

eventually," I said.

"Me too. I hope they stay safe for what could be ahead of them."

"Me too, Jasper."

Chapter 15

A close call

Sandy led the way using the scale that came from Jasper, and Atom and Jayjay followed close behind.

Jayjay and Atom looked around the unfamiliar surroundings they'd been thrown into by the current far behind them, lost in curiosity. Atom took snapshots of the plants that caught his eye the most, even collecting tiny samples of sea plants and moss and keeping them in his chest cavity to study later.

As they progressed further, they came across a Kelp Forest. However, this Kelp Forest was extraordinary; the yellowy-green kelp stretched more than a hundred metres up to the water's surface as they coiled with each other to look like chains. Near or just under the surface of the water, smaller vines with clusters of glowing yellow seeds were seen swaying with the gentle current. Some creatures latched onto the kelp to sleep, eat the yellow pods, or play, while others grabbed rocks to poke purple sea urchins on the seabed.

Those creatures looked like a mixture of a monkey, an otter, and a fish, and they came in a variety of colours. There were webbed dorsal fins on their heads and two bigger majestic fins in between, and their cheeks had freckles. They had four arms and a tail that stretched a metre and a half. They had black sparkling eyes and mesmerising patterns of stripes on their arms, and their tails were another colour.

"They're so cute!" Jayjay almost squealed.

"What are these creatures? They look like Sea Monkeys," Sandy said.

"They must be, due to their behaviour," Atom replied.

"How so?"

"They are smart enough to use rocks as tools to open the shells of sea urchins."

"I guess that makes sense; you are the expert on anemone."

Atom was confused as to what she meant. "'Anemone'?"

Sandy took a moment to find the right words to tell him what she meant. "Y'know…the thing where you look at a living being's insides to learn their functions?"

Atom now understood. "That's called anatomy, not anemone. I'm talking about adaptation and evolution."

"Whatever you call it, Tester," she sighed.

A few moments later, the Sea Monkeys saw them and approached from the kelp and seabed around them.

Sandy noticed them coming and brought Jayjay and Atom close to her back, shielding them with her aquatic wings.

Atom peeked over Sandy's arm and then chuckled as one of the creatures came closer to them, showing a curious expression in its eyes towards Sandy.

"Why's it looking at me like that?" Sandy asked Atom, confused.

"It's checking you out. From my understanding, it's never seen a Batfish before."

"Well, none of us have ever seen a Sea Monkey before, but I wouldn't be curious."

More Sea Monkeys approached them, sniffing their mysterious scent in the water. Some swam around them, and one grabbed Sandy's arm and faced Atom. It tilted its head right as it flapped its two long, blue, luscious fins over its face.

"Why, hello there," Atom said to the Sea Monkey.

The Sea Monkey just stared at him, not knowing what he said. It noticed the red metal balls behind his drone head, and the fins between its face began vibrating. It wanted to grab Atom with all four of its hands, but Sandy quickly prevented it from doing so.

"Don't even think about it, Sea Monkey!" Sandy snarled.

The Sea Monkey backed away, but then its attention was caught by the glimmering scale she was holding in her hand. The other Sea Monkeys saw it too, and their eyes sparkled with its beauty as they came closer to Sandy, Atom, and Jayjay.

Noticing their behaviour, Jayjay asked, "Um…is it just me, or are they coming towards us?"

Confused and alarmed at the same time, Sandy replied, "Okay, this is treacherous behaviour coming from these critters, and I don't like it."

Atom looked all around the approaching Sea

Monkeys until he realised their eyes were locked onto the scale in Sandy's hand. He quickly snatched the scale, opened his chest cavity, and chucked it inside before closing it.

Now more confused by what Atom had just done, she asked, "Why did you do that? What's going on with their treacherous behaviour?"

"It's not treacherous behaviour...they want the scale!" Atom warned her.

The Sea Monkeys all saw what happened, and their eyes locked onto Atom, showing their razor-sharp teeth and raising their arms at him.

"Those are some angry Sea Monkeys! *Swim for your life!*" Atom screamed.

Sandy quickly grabbed Atom, moved him onto her stomach, and wrapped one of her wings over him, securing him in place and shielding him from the Sea Monkeys. Jayjay quickly came and wrapped her tentacles over Sandy's body as she dashed away from the aggravated Sea Monkeys that began chasing after them.

"This is our scale! You'll never take us alive!" Sandy shouted at them.

The Sea Monkeys chased them through the biome as they started growing their numbers drastically from all directions. Sandy tried to shake them off by slipping through the giant chain-looking kelp, where only a few Sea Monkeys got tangled in the roots and stalks.

The rest of the swarm went around them.

After a few twists and turns to avoid getting tangled in the kelp, Sandy started to slow down due to her other wing holding Atom, as she used both her aquatic wings to dash through the water.

As the Sea Monkeys began to gain on them, Jayjay noticed, from the corner of her left eye, a nearby green hill with a sizeable purple-dark cave that had glowing yellow pods growing just outside the entrance. She pointed and shouted, "There's a cave on our left!"

Sandy saw the cave and immediately went to it. "In we go! I hope they're scared of the dark!"

When they entered the cave, the Sea Monkeys behind them stopped as fear seemed to creep into their faces, and they fled, screeching and yelling.

The three friends noticed, and Sandy shouted at the Sea Monkeys, "That's right! You better swim away, you little scale-snatchers!"

Suddenly, a moment later, the cave closed over them, and everything was engulfed by darkness. The only lights that shone were Jayjay's body and Sandy's bioluminescence in her tail and wings.

Jayjay unravelled her tentacles from her as she let go of Atom.

"Why did it just get so dark?" Sandy asked, stunned by what had just happened. "That is not what a cave is supposed to do."

Her voice echoed through the cave.

"Is it just me, or does this cave sound… alive?" Atom asked.

"'Alive' meaning that we aren't in a cave at all?" Sandy's pupils constricted drastically as she thought about that.

They heard a nearby pulse, and the cave started

to move slightly.

When it stopped, Sandy turned and glared at Jayjay. "Jayjay, I swear to the goddess, if you just led us into a creature's mouth."

Jayjay chuckled nervously. "Sorry, Sandy."

"*That is not going to cut it!*"

"Whoa, Sandy! Cease your rage! That's not gonna fix it! Let's remain calm and find a way out of here," Atom murmured to himself, gently tapping his metal head.

"I can use my spines," Sandy suggested, pointing at the long spines on her head.

But Atom shook his head worriedly. "That's not a good idea. We'll be moved down its gullet if you do that anywhere in its mouth, especially the tongue!"

Sandy was speechless for a moment. "*Oh! And what about it? Do you want it to swallow us eventually? I don't want to be in the stomach of a predator! That is the last thing all of us want!*"

As Atom and Sandy started to argue, the water around them began to drain, bringing them down until they were on the slimy, squishy ground.

When Jayjay's body softly landed on the creature's tongue, the taste buds began to make a sizzling sound, and everything started shaking dramatically again.

Sandy and Atom stopped arguing and held onto the tongue firmly.

"What is happening? Why is everything moving?" Sandy exclaimed, confused and worried at the same time.

The shaking grew stronger until their grip slipped

off, and they slammed against the creature's pointy teeth. Next, they were thrown onto the roof of the mouth and landed back down on the tongue. Then everything moved up diagonally so that Sandy, Atom and Jayjay had to hold onto the tongue to avoid falling down the throat.

The creature slightly opened its mouth, and light and the view of the water's surface were revealed before a powerful gust of air rushed in, forcing Sandy, Jayjay, and Atom towards the creature's throat.

"I don't wanna die!" Sandy screamed.

But then, instead of being pushed into the creature's stomach, they were blown out of a blowhole from on top of the creature's head, and the three friends flew high up into the air, screaming at the top of their lungs, even as they fell, splashing back into the water.

After slowly sinking until they came to a stop, the creature they had been spat out of descended from the surface and swam away.

It was a green leviathan with a kelp-like appearance to camouflage with the kelp around it and yellow bioluminescence on its underside and around its mouth.

Everyone was speechless for a moment.

Finally, Atom spoke, "So we were in the mouth of a leviathan."

"We're alive! I thought we were gonna die! But no! We lived!" Sandy laughed, overjoyed and relieved they were free. She hugged Atom as she spun.

However, Jayjay wasn't overjoyed; she had a mix

of emotions as she watched the leviathan disappear into the underwater wilderness. She then looked at her blue-tipped tentacles and remembered what caused the leviathan to spit them out.

Was that…from me? Did I save us?

When Sandy turned to Jayjay, still laughing, her smile slowly turned to a frown, and she let go of Atom before approaching her. "Jayjay? Are you okay?"

"I…don't know. When I was on the leviathan's tongue, it started to swell, and it made it sound like it was in pain that it spat us out. Did I do that?"

Sandy thought about that, then realised that Jayjay had saved them all without knowing. Her smile returned, and she wrapped her wings around Jayjay, squeezing her gently with gratitude.

"If you made the creature spit us out by burning its tongue, then yes, you saved us. I didn't know you had a defence mechanism."

Jayjay tilted her head. "What's a defence mechanism?"

Sandy let go of her and held one of her tentacles. "It's something a lot of creatures have to say to their predators, *'Don't eat me; I'm not food'*. It protects them by either being poisonous, shooting chemicals at them, or anything that helps them survive. My defence mechanisms are my spines, speed and bite."

Jayjay's eyes sparkled as she learned she had a defence mechanism.

Then Sandy added, "To be honest, I'm glad you had a defence mechanism that causes mouths to burn. If it weren't for you, then we would've been digested.

I'm sorry I was being hard on you earlier. I get tense, and I don't even realise it sometimes."

"It's okay, Sandy. I do remember you saying that when we first met."

She paused for a moment. Then replied, "You know, you and I will make great friends, and you'll definitely get along with my best friend, Barbara."

"That sounds lovely. But we still need to find Jasper, Charlie and Lulu."

She nodded, agreeing with Jayjay. "Then what are we waiting for? Atom! You still have the scale in your chest cavity?"

Atom nodded as he pressed the top of his chest cavity, opened it, and took out the scale. "Safe and sound! Now that we aren't being chased by Sea Monkeys and not in the mouth of a leviathan anymore, let's keep searching!"

Sandy took the scale, sniffed it to resume the path, and they all made a move through the biome. Atom quickly grabbed onto her spines.

They made their way through the Kelp Forest until the ground came to a stop at deeper waters, where dunes greeted them. Staring down at the dunes, a nervous feeling filled their bodies.

Sandy's muscles tensed. From her eyes, the fading scent was leading down. To double-check, she took another smell of Jasper's scale, and her instinct was correct.

Atom and Jayjay looked at her.

"They got to be down there somewhere; the path is showing me they're down there," Sandy said.

"I hope they're still okay," Jayjay replied worriedly.

Then, from a far distance, they heard the sound of a whale.

"What's that noise?" Jayjay asked.

"That's a whale song. I've always wondered what it sounded like for a long time," Sandy answered, her nervousness quickly fading away as she listened to the song, and a feeling of peace filled her and Jayjay.

"It sounds... beautiful, like a lullaby of the sea," Jayjay said.

"Agreed," Sandy replied.

After a calming moment of listening to the whale song, Sandy decided to resume the search, so she sniffed the scale again to reveal the path and told Jayjay and Atom to follow her as they began to descend from the Kelp Forest.

This was new territory they were about to enter, and they wondered what they could find below.

Hopefully, Charlie, Jasper, and Lulu will be there at some point in the deep.

Chapter 16

A call to the whales

Jasper and I continuously made our way through the dunes. However, by the time we finished swimming over every hill of sand, Jasper started slowing down and couldn't keep up. I stopped to let him catch his breath when I noticed.

Lulu stopped, too, and looked at him.

I was surprised Jasper was exhausted from swimming because I wasn't at all. "You alright?" I asked.

Jasper looked at me. "I'm…I'm alright. I'm just tired from kicking my feet repeatedly. How do you keep up that much?"

I shrugged. "I dunno. I don't feel tired. Maybe it's because of my powers."

"Makes sense." Jasper gradually sank to the sand below to rest his tired legs as he took deep breaths to regain his energy.

I don't feel tired, Lulu said with her telepathy.

For a moment, I looked at the pod of Blue-Spotted Whales as they swam faster than us. Worry began to fill me. I said to myself, "We're not gonna keep up with them. We'll lose them in less than a minute!"

I knew I had to keep us going.

I could carry Jasper to follow the whales to reach our destination, which was still very far away. But I didn't want to use my speed, or I would accidentally hurt Jasper. There had to be another way, and I needed to think quickly before the whales disappeared into the blue. I closed my eyes and went into deep thought, even pressing my webbed fingers against my head. *C'mon, Charlie. Think of something to catch us up to the whales!*

Don't stress your mind too much, Orla said.

I try not to, Orla. But this is an emergency!

I thought as hard as I could to hatch a plan to catch up to the whales.

But then I felt something tapping between my eyes. I opened them and saw Lulu in front of me with a wide grin on her face.

I have an idea!

Surprise filled me when she said that confidently. "You do? What's your idea, Lulu?"

I have another power, and I used it to save you back in the Kelp Forest! Maybe I can get the whales to come to us!

I was a bit unsure at first. But then the memory of the bright flash that stopped Pearl from eating me and Atom popped into my head, convincing me that it would actually work by how powerful the flash was.

Orla thought Lulu was right. *Her flash of light should be just bright enough to get their attention. They will surely help!*

"Was that what that flash of light was?" Jasper asked.

Lulu nodded at him.

 I replied confidently.

Lulu nodded, and then she swam away to space herself from us. She closed her eyes, tucked her fins to her body and made straining noises to focus on her light.

Jasper and I watched as she steadily charged up her flash. At one moment, she opened her eyes and panted from exhaustion. But she didn't give up and grew brighter the more she focused. She tried harder, even holding her breath so that her cheeks blew up like balloons.

You may need to cover your eyes; she's almost charged to flash her light, Orla suggested.

Jasper and I did just that.

Finally, she released a massive flash of light that lasted a few seconds, along with a high-pitched cry. Jasper and I were lucky Orla told us to protect our eyes, or we would've only seen white.

After Lulu's light dimmed, we uncovered our eyes and looked at the distant whales, hoping we caught their attention in time.

The whales had stopped. That increased our hope of whether the flash actually worked.

Then, a moment later, the whales slowly turned around and headed towards us as they sang their song!

Excitement struck us and we laughed.

"It worked!" I shouted.

"I can't believe that worked! That's incredible!" Jasper exclaimed.

As the whales grew closer, one of them stopped in front of us. We swam directly to it and gently placed our hands on its snout.

Jasper seemed so amazed as if he had never seen a whale before that he moved his hand back and forth on the whale's skin.

Finally, I swam to the whale's left eye, sliding my hands over its skin along the way, and asked, "Is it alright that we hitch a ride? We are trying to get to the Deep Spirit Tree to return one of Orla's young, and we're looking for our friends at the same time."

The whale took a moment to think. Then, slowly, it lowered its head down for us to hop on. Jasper and Lulu went on, and I smiled gratefully at the whale. "Thank you!"

Its huge eye showed a look of kindness.

Finally, I joined Jasper and Lulu.

The whales turned around and swam to the surface, followed by the one we were on, continuing their journey with us.

A whole mix of emotions was inside me, and it was too difficult to explain which one I was feeling. I had never ridden on top of a whale before! I looked at Jasper as he stared back at me; he must've been feeling the same as I was. He held Lulu in his hand, and she squealed and laughed like she was having fun!

We laughed with her. Eventually, we calmed down.

"Now, this is easier than kicking our feet a million times," I said.

Jasper agreed. Then his smile slowly turned into a frown as he faced the whale's skin.

Noticing his change of expression, I asked, "Are you okay?"

"I miss my best friend. It already feels like forever, and I'm worried about whether we'll ever find her again."

An empathetic smirk crossed over my face, knowing how much he missed her. "It'll be alright, Jasper, I promise. We will find our friends at some point; we just need to stay strong and keep searching."

His smile was restored when I said that, and he nodded.

As time went by, the sun was beginning to set. There was only deep blue below us, and the whales kept going, singing their song.

They slowly moved closer to the surface to catch a breath, but the one we were in decided to bring us up completely out of the water. As we were risen out of the water, I quickly used my water ability to create a floating water ball with Lulu swimming inside.

Finally, we emerged from the water completely, dripping and wet.

The whale's blowhole behind me blew water up into the air, and it sprinkled over us, keeping us moist.

Lulu giggled because of the noise of the blowhole.

Jasper looked around in amazement, his eyes sparkling as if he had never seen what it looked like from out of the water before. But then, a few seconds later, his skin started to burn, and he tucked his arms to his chest. I quickly realised he was in pain, and I used my water powers to cover his body in water.

"Are you okay?" I asked him.

He nodded. "I'm okay. Just a little burnt."

"I didn't know that could happen!" I replied.

I never told either of you this, but Mersinganoids are so sensitive to high temperatures that they could die from it.

Our eyes widened when Orla told us this.

"Why didn't you tell us earlier?" I asked Orla.

"So that must be why," I heard Jasper say to himself.

I looked at him, surprised. "That wasn't the first time?"

"No. When I was younger, I wanted to try to get out of the water before, but when I tried raising my hand out of the water, it felt like it was boiling, so I brought it back down. I tried a few times but never succeeded, and I didn't know why I kept getting myself burnt. So finally, I decided to stay in the water," he said.

"You wanted to explore my land?" I asked.

He nodded. "I wanted to, but I thought it was best not to risk myself getting burnt again."

My eyebrows furrowed when I heard all of this, and a sense of empathy filled my stomach. Then I asked, "What about the cenote?"

"You mean where I found you for the first time? I even tried there, but I still got burnt."

"I'm…so sorry to hear, Jasper. Have you ever tried at night?"

"I'm too worried to go out again, even at night," he answered.

I thought about it for a moment, then I glanced at the setting sun behind me, then up in the sky, as I began to notice the first star appearing.

"Well...why don't we try when it becomes night time?"

Jasper's eyebrows creased and a look of concern crept on his face. "I don't know about this."

"It'll be okay, trust me. Though, I'll have to keep myself wet because after some time, I'll change back to normal."

His cheek fins went up when he heard that. "I thought that was your original form."

"This is my aquatic form. I transform when I come in contact with water. This is my first elemental form."

"That's amazing!" he said softly, smiling.

I smiled at him. "It won't be long until night arrives," I replied, turning around to watch the setting sun.

Jasper crawled over to watch too as he held the ball of water with Lulu inside.

"It's beautiful, isn't it?" I asked.

"It really is! If only Jayjay could see this!"

"Sometimes, back on my ship, I would come to the shipyard and watch the sunset with Chuckboi. I bet he's watching it, too," I softly said.

"I bet he's right now, thinking about you," Jasper replied.

My eyes narrowed as I looked at the whale's skin, which had a few small and large barnacles that had holes big enough that Lulu could swim in. I sighed deeply.

You miss everyone, don't you?

I nodded. "I do, Orla, but I'm not stopping until we find our friends and return Lulu to you."

You have great confidence in you, Charlie.

I can't wait to go home, Lulu said telepathically. Then she yawned.

Jasper and I looked at her as she slowly closed her eyes to sleep. Carefully, I controlled the floating water with her in it, moving her off Jasper's hand and into a large barnacle with a hole deep enough for her to fit and rest, and dropped her in before I continued watching the sunset.

Eventually, the sun went under the ocean horizon and the Silver Moon shone in the sky as thousands of stars twinkled.

Lulu was fast asleep in the harmless barnacle.

The water I kept on Jasper's body to prevent him from burning remained as I had to splash myself from changing back to normal.

I finally thought it was time for Jasper to get out of his comfort zone and experience what it looks like out of the water.

"Alright, Jasper. It's dark enough, and I should be able to move the water off you. Are you ready?" I asked.

Jasper stuttered for a moment. "I'm very nervous."

"It's okay, Jasper. I'm right here, and I'll make sure you are okay, okay?"

He stared at me for another moment, and then finally, he nodded after taking a deep breath. "Okay…I'm ready. Move the water off me."

I smiled and nodded back. Then, I gradually moved

the water down from Jasper, starting from his head. As the water moved, he closed his eyes until it reached his chest. He opened his eyes barely to see what was happening to him, and they widened as the water went down his chest, arms, hands and finally down his crossed legs.

His body was dripping, and he looked at his hands, a mix of shock and amazement in his eyes. "I'm not burning!"

I chuckled. "Told you I was here to make sure you were okay!"

"And I still am! Thank you," he said as his smile became soft.

"No problem. Now look up to the sky, and tell me what you see," I said as I looked up.

He did just that, and I heard him gasp. "It's…it's…I can't describe how beautiful it looks! So much clearer!"

"It's very beautiful, isn't it?"

"It truly is!"

I lay down on the whale's skin as I watched the stars. "I still remember my first time seeing the Silver Moon. Chuckboi showed it to me from higher above the trees when we were young."

"The moon always looks distorted from under the water. Now it's still and looks like a giant pearl."

I laughed. "Does it?"

"Yeah!" he replied as he laughed with me.

When I calmed down, I yawned. "Pardon me. I'm sleepy."

"That's okay. Why don't I sing you to sleep?" Jasper asked.

"Do whatever you want that makes you happy," I replied.

I would love to listen to your song, Jasper, as would my Golden Starpearl.

Jasper nodded as he must've heard what Orla said and began to sing.

Hearing his voice again really soothed me to the point that I could barely open my eyes as my mind went to sleep under his song.

The whales stopped their song to listen to him.

I smiled in my sleep as I felt a hand, most likely Jasper's, gently stroking my left arm as he sang.

Slowly and eventually, the sounds around me silenced as I went into a deep sleep.

Chapter 17

Dawn had returned to Hybrainia once again.

I had slept peacefully on the whale's back that still protruded from the water, thanks to Jasper's beautiful singing.

I sat up and stretched my arms as I yawned. "Morning, Jasper. Morning, Lulu."

Strangely, I heard no response.

I opened my eyes and saw I had changed back to my normal form, and Jasper and Lulu weren't around. My fatigue immediately went away, and I worried about where they were.

"Jasper?" I called out.

But there was no response.

"Lulu?" I cried.

No response from her either.

My worry grew as if they had been left behind until I was suddenly splashed by water from behind, which changed me back into my water form. I turned around and saw a bright gold light and a faint turquoise and blue figure under the water.

It was Jasper and Lulu!

I sighed with relief.

"There you are! You almost gave me a heart

attack!" I said.

"I wanted to let you know we are under the water. I started to burn, so I went under, taking Lulu with me," Jasper replied.

I thought that it was understandable and I said to myself, "Why should I be mad? Of course, he's sensitive to heat!"

Soon, the whale we were on went under the water, and I submerged with it.

Because I was very warm from the sunlight, the water felt so cold! Fortunately, I got used to it very quickly.

Jasper and Lulu came back up to me, and we sat there for a while, not knowing what to do.

Then, after some time, the pod of Blue-Spotted Whales dove down near the surface, and we held on, confused as to where we were going.

As the whales went further down, we began to notice a massive vine with enormous glowing blue polyps.

A nervous feeling flowed in our bodies like currents as we sensed it was something huge!

Suddenly, a massive school of fish escaped from the deep blue, swimming in the opposite direction of us! They went past us so fast that we almost lost our grip on the whales as we continued down.

"What's going on?" I stammered.

"I don't know!" Jasper stammered back as he held Lulu close to him.

There's something down there that's hunting for them! You need to stay clear of it!

Suddenly, a large group of sparkling lights rose from the deep, and the vine went down.

The whales stopped diving and continued forward. As they did, the sparkling lights grew in numbers until an enormous figure emerged from the darkness, chasing after the school of fish!

Me and Jasper screamed at the top of our lungs as the giant beast rose at great speed!

Thanks to the whales, we just managed to avoid its huge mouth as it broke the surface. Its three huge eyes passed us, and then a pectoral fin with a glowing white lining cut through the water.

A moment later, the giant beast stopped swimming upward as if it had caught its meal, and it stayed there, its mouth right on the surface, for a long time.

We watched in shock, and we barely avoided the beast as it slowly began to sink back down into the water.

The pod of whales swam swiftly until the creature's head was under the water.

By the look of its appearance, it seemed to be like a giant whale shark.

I couldn't help but smile upon seeing this humongous beast as it began swimming back into the depths of the sea. We kept watching it until we could only see its tail and the sparkling lights as the tentacle from earlier rose back up.

Jasper and I looked at each other and started laughing nervously.

"That was close!" he exclaimed.

Jasper just kept laughing as he couldn't find his

words after that close experience.

What was that thing? It was huge…and hungry, Lulu said telepathically.

That was a Colossal Twilight Shark! I don't see them very often from my Deep Spirit Tree. They camouflage themselves within the floating Sea Stars of the Twilight Zone. Their eyesight is poor, so they rely on their two tentacles, one floating above while the other hangs below. The tentacle that floats has polyps that act as sensors, which detect vibrations from above, sending signals to its brain that it is either a school of fish, which they feast on, or other sea creatures that they will leave alone, like whales. The other tentacle doesn't have those polyps. Instead, it detects the temperatures from below. If it's cold, then it is alright for now. If it is hot, then the shark would avoid it as that tentacle is sensitive and could hurt it.

Interesting! It looks like a whale shark that I've been told about by the fishermen back in Pollen Village!

It is a relative of the shark family that lives in the deep.

That's incredible!

It is, indeed.

"Sometimes, back in my reef, we'd get smaller whale sharks from the dunes. The fish, wrasse and I would help clean them of parasites that had latched onto their bodies. Sometimes Jayjay and I eat them when we're hungry," Jasper said; he must've also heard what she said in his mind.

"How often do you get them in your reef?" I asked him.

He shrugged. "Most of the time, just one or two, and they are completely different from the one we've just seen."

Lulu looked up at him and asked verbally, "Parasites? What are those?"

"They are small creatures that latch onto a host, either to suck their nutrients or blood. I once had a few stuck in my mouth, but the wrasse took great care of me," he answered.

"Did it hurt when you had parasites inside your mouth, skin and scales?" I asked.

"Depends on the parasite, but yes; it itched and felt like they were digging into my scales," he said as he moved his hand over his right shoulder scales. But then he must've noticed something was off and glanced at his shoulder. "Oh. I lost one."

"You lost one?" I said, tilting my head. I crawled closer to see.

Jasper moved Lulu in his other hand to let her have a look, and she covered her mouth.

One of his big shoulder scales was gone, leaving a gap on his shoulder.

"Does it hurt when you lose a scale?" I asked.

"Not really; it happens every now and then. A lot of the sea creatures in my reef find my scales attractive, and I don't blame them," he replied.

"Not gonna lie, you do have very beautiful scales," I complimented.

He smiled at me, and his chest started glowing,

faintly revealing his beating heart. "Thank you."

Lulu noticed his glowing heart and stared at it as her eyes grew wide, and she slowly moved her tiny fins away from her mouth.

Jasper looked at her and noticed she was staring at his glowing heart. "Are you staring at my heart, Lulu?"

She didn't say anything, but then reached her tiny fins out to touch his chest.

She wants to hear your heart, Jasper, Orla spoke in our minds.

He understood and gently brought Lulu close to his chest as her tiny fin hands touched his scales, listening to every beat inside him. The sound must've soothed her so much that she closed her eyes.

The sound of a Mersinganoid's heart is so familiar.

"Does it, Lulu?" Jasper asked.

She nodded.

The Mersinganoids did the same to you before you were born; their words were all sweet. They brought you close to their hearts to share their love with you as they said their words. They even sang to you, Lulu.

We noticed Lulu smile as Orla spoke telepathically. Then she said, "I hope Jayjay...and Sandy...are okay."

"We will reunite with them at some point; we just need to keep searching and moving. Pearl might be after us, but we will protect you from her, Lulu, we promise," I replied.

Jasper agreed.

Lulu opened her eyes and glanced at me, still smiling. "Thank you, Charwie and Japper."

We nodded at her and turned in the direction of the Blue-Spotted Whales swimming.

I know they're out there somewhere; we just need to keep going and searching. Sandy? Atom? Wherever you two are, I hope we'll find each other and complete this mission.

I released a deep sigh, and my eyes narrowed as I was already missing them. *I hope we find each other soon.*

Chapter 18

The search for more clues

Sandy, Atom and Jayjay searched the sand dunes for hours. Sandy didn't sleep, while Jayjay and Atom did. She continuously sniffed the water, following Jasper's scent like a path only she could see, using the scale Atom caught back in the currents.

Jayjay rested her body on Sandy's back with her tentacles wrapped around her spines. She was looking around the sandy hills as an uneasy feeling flowed through her body. Atom felt the same.

"Um… Is it just me, or does it feel a bit… too calm?" Jayjay asked.

"From what I know back in the Crystal Dunes, they're meant to be calm… I hope," Sandy replied. "The scent is powerful around here. They must've been here."

Jayjay's eyes lit up. "Then that means they've got to be close! A strong scent is good, right?"

"Yes! I hope they're alright!" she replied as she started calling out for them. "Charlie! Jasper! Where are you? Can you hear me?"

Her voice echoed through the water.

But there was no response.

Sandy shouted again. "Charlie? Jasper?"

Still nothing.

Jayjay's optimism began to fade as the only things they heard were the whale songs and the distant bubbles. But Sandy was certain they had to be nearby, so she sniffed the scale again. Her hindsight showed distorted, transparent figures of Jasper, Charlie, and Lulu swimming in the same direction as they were.

"I can see the figures of Charlie, Jasper and Lulu right in front of me, moving in the same direction as we are right now. It must seem like they were trying to follow something," Sandy said.

"Like what?" Atom asked.

"I don't know yet. Perhaps, maybe at some point, whatever they might have been trying to follow, it shows me," she replied.

Atom sighed heavily and murmured to himself, "Oh dear goddess, I hope we find them and that they are alright. I will never forgive Pearl for what she did."

Sandy heard him. "I feel the exact same way as you, Atom. I hope she gets a taste of her own medicine."

Jayjay overheard her words and asked, "What is medicine?"

"It's an expression; it means that I hope she gets karma," she answered.

"Oh," Jayjay replied as her eyes narrowed. She laid her head down on Sandy's back and released a deep sigh.

"You good?" Sandy asked.

"I miss my best friend. I've never been away from him, ever," she answered softly.

Sandy was surprised. "You've never been away from him?"

"Not even once. I grew up always close to him. I feel vulnerable without him; I feel like I can't fend for myself, even though I now know I have a defence mechanism. He's like a big brother to me; he keeps me safe, healthy and free of parasites."

Sandy looked at the sand below her as she swam. "I know how you feel, Jayjay. But Batfish, such as myself, are born to fend for themselves. I felt incomplete as I didn't have any friends back then. I was born in a lake where swans once migrated, and the rest of my kind had already gone, leaving only the eggs they hatched from behind. My sight was much worse back then; I only saw black and white, which is unnatural for my kind. But as I grew older and found my friends, my vision managed to change, and I could just faintly see a few colours, but not all correctly."

"You have said that before. I never knew that was a thing," Jayjay said.

"Tritanopia Colour Blindness is when you don't see colours properly. I can only see blues and pinks. The two pupils of my kind have allowed us to track things from scent, and the smaller pupils act as our hindsight, giving us an idea of what had happened in the past. My eyes didn't develop properly before birth, causing me to go colour-blind, but my hindsight definitely has."

Jayjay's eyes narrowed when she heard that. "I'm so sorry. That must've been tough for you."

"Oh, don't be; I may not see colours the way you do, but I can still recognise shapes, sounds, voices and faces. I have great friends who help me with colours," Sandy replied with a positive smirk.

Jayjay's frown turned into a smile, and she stroked her blue-tipped tentacle over Sandy's forehead. "You also have me."

Sandy laughed. "Yes, I have you too, Jayjay…and Atom."

Atom nodded, even though he wasn't paying attention.

Sandy repeatedly sniffed the scale to follow the distorted figures of Charlie, Jasper, and Lulu until they came to a stop. Jasper was so exhausted that he sank onto the sand, where a pair of footprints were visible.

Sandy stopped, as Atom did too.

"Why did you stop?" Jayjay asked.

"It shows to me that the three of them stopped in this exact spot," Sandy replied.

Jayjay leaned over to see the footprints, and her eyes lit up as she gasped. Then she hopped off her and swam straight to the footprints.

Atom was so confused by her behaviour that he came to investigate, too, using his scanning to survey the area. It picked up the footprints. "Footprints! They must've been here earlier!" he exclaimed.

The distorted figures of Charlie, Jasper and Lulu faded away from Sandy's eyes as she approached the footprints, her hope growing considerably. "From my eyes, Jasper sat down because he was exhausted from swimming, leaving his imprint. But the scent also stops here!" Sandy said.

Jayjay and Atom both looked at her.

"If his scent stopped here, then why?" Atom asked.

"I'm about to find out," she said as she took another sniff from the scale, bringing back the distorted figures of the three of them.

Charlie was frantically looking back from Jasper and to the open ocean for some reason until Lulu's expression became positive; she must've used her telepathy to communicate with them.

By the sudden change in Lulu's expression, Sandy recognised that she had an idea. She kept observing with her hindsight until Charlie and Jasper swam away from Lulu by a couple of metres.

Okay, so Lulu had an idea; could she recognise what she was doing from her face? Sandy wondered.

Then, Lulu began to curl her tiny fins to her body as if she were charging herself, and she started becoming brighter and brighter. One moment, she was exhausted, but continued to charge herself until a bright flash of light escaped her body.

Because of how sudden the flash was to Sandy, it made her jump and gasp. She didn't need to cover her eyes as it was from the past, and the light was fainter.

"What's wrong? What are you seeing? What's happening from your eyes? Tell us!" Jayjay asked repeatedly, eager to know what was going on.

"Just calm down, Jayjay. I'll tell you once I know everything that has happened!" Sandy exclaimed.

When the light dimmed, showing Lulu, Jasper, and Charlie again, they watched the distant ocean for a moment, then became highly excited and swam to…whatever they were overjoyed about.

Sandy watched until they came to a stop, as if they were in front of something, before Jasper and Lulu hopped onto the mysterious being. Charlie swam to its side to potently caress it before joining the others, and they were taken into the far ocean.

After that, the hindsight faded away.

"Where did they go now?" Atom asked, facing the same direction Sandy was.

She turned back to him. "Lulu charged up her light to probably catch the attention of something. I don't know what, but it must've been huge if it looked like they were being carried away by whatever they aimed for."

Atom took in all of the information Sandy had told him, and he pondered.

"Something big?" Jayjay asked, slowly becoming worried. "I hope it wasn't Pearl!"

"It isn't anything like that; they were excited about it. Whatever it was that took them into the distant ocean, it had to be friendly."

"Friendly and huge..." Atom murmured as he pondered.

Then, the sounds of whales from above were heard, and they all faced up, seeing a pod of Blue-Spotted Whales.

"I think we have our answer," Atom replied, grinning widely.

"I don't see anything," Sandy answered, searching for the whales as her colour blindness made it hard to see them.

Atom came to her and pointed his metal hand to

show where the pod was. "They're right there. Try squinting your eyes."

Sandy squinted her eyes. "Oh, now I see them, just barely."

"Whales must've taken them! Maybe they can help us too!" Jayjay shouted gleefully.

"But what direction do they go?" Sandy asked.

"From what I've heard back in Pollen Village, they travel south to feast in the summertime, and in the winter, they travel north to breed," Atom answered.

"Now *that* is useful for getting us closer to finding our friends. Maybe they'll allow us to hitch a ride like they did for them! C'mon!" She started swimming towards the whales. Atom and Jayjay followed her.

As they got closer to the passing whales, Sandy shouted to them to get their attention. "*Hey! Down here! Wait!*"

"Be careful, Sandy: they have very powerful pectoral fins!" Atom reminded her.

"I will!" she shouted back as she approached the whale's right eye.

The whale's eye faced her, and she smiled nervously as if it were a vast being.

"Hey! Do you mind if we hitch a ride? We're trying to look for our friends; we got separated back in the Deep Blue currents, and we're searching for them. Is that okay with you?"

The whale's eye stared at her for a moment before slowly shifting back to where it was going.

"Was that a yes or a no?" Sandy asked kindly, waiting for a response.

Then the whale slowly spun over onto its belly, and the top of its pectoral fin caught Atom, Jayjay, and Sandy as they spun with it before the whale went back up. They held onto its fin with surprise.

"Wasn't expecting that kind of response, but I'll take it as a 'yes'," Sandy said.

Jayjay laughed with joy as they rode the whale, taking them with the rest of the pod into the distant waters. "We're coming for you, Jasper, Lulu and Charlie!"

Chapter 19

Time drifted away as the whales we were on took us into further unknown waters. The sun had moved to the east, nearing the ocean's horizon again.

I was sitting near the Blue-Spotted whale's snout while Jasper and Lulu remained on its back behind me.

He was quietly humming his gentle song to Lulu, who was tucked in his hands, asleep. Even from near the whale's snout, my eyes were very heavy, and I nearly nodded off a few times. I thought it was so incredible for Jasper and his species to be born with such beautiful voices that can calm the ocean's creatures, even me and Orla and her young.

I turned my body to face Jasper and watched as he slowly rocked Lulu, making her smile in her sleep. I smiled at him, even as his heart began to glow.

I can sense that his heart is so pure and gentle to all creatures of the ocean, no matter what they are, Orla spoke in my head.

I faintly nodded. *You can even see it glow. It reminds me of someone from a cold tundra who had a pure and caring heart.*

Oh? Were they a Mersinganoid, too?

No. He was a different species who had adapted

to the cold earlier this year and found his first love there. He also had the voice of an angel.

That sounds like he is a charming land person.

He's married now; he has wanted that for years, and we helped him bring that wish to reality.

That is a great deed of yours, Charlie.

He needed our help, too, because way before he was married and even met his partner, he was banished from my island and was blown all the way to the tundra.

Orla gasped in shock. *By whom?*

A menace to society.

Fair answer.

I sighed deeply and looked down to my left of the whale and noticed something was off further below. I swam to the whale's pectoral fin and grabbed on as I began to see pointy hills spewing gas and bubbles up to the surface.

What's wrong? What are you seeing below? Orla asked in my head.

I squinted my eyes to get a better look, even stretching my hand down to feel the water's temperature.

"The water here is warm," I said to myself, *"that's…odd. Orla? Would you know what this is?"*

The temperature began to rise above my body and the whale until I heard Jasper stop singing and making painful grunts. I turned and saw he had jumped off the whale and swam for cooler water higher above. I quickly hopped off the whale and went straight for him as the pod left us behind in this mysterious, warm place.

"Jasper! Are you okay?" I asked as I finally came to him.

I noticed a few of his scales had turned darker than before, as a few from his arms had fallen off.

My eyes widened in shock, as did Lulu's when she noticed, even covering her mouth.

Jasper looked at his missing scales, then smirked with a nervous chuckle. "I'm okay, Charlie and Lulu. I'm just a little burnt. It's nothing."

"Jasper, you are temperature-sensitive! If the temperature gets too great, you'll die!" I exclaimed.

It's true, Jasper! Your kind isn't adapted to extremely warm biomes such as this! Orla spoke in our heads. *Even worse, this place stretches for kilometres. The only way to pass here is to go through!*

Annoyance filled me as I somehow knew Orla would say that. "Of course, we have to go through."

Suddenly, one of the nearby thermal vents further down from us exploded, releasing a massive cloud of black smoke and rocks into the water. We jumped in fright from the sudden noise and watched as the black cloud rose to the surface, making the water around us feel warmer.

I heard Jasper making grunting noises, so I looked at him again to see his skin tingling, more scales falling off, and pink areas beginning to form. I grabbed his hand and examined his skin as it slowly began to peel and turn dark.

"Jasper! This is serious! We have to go before you

boil too much and die from the heat!" I exclaimed.

But then, after a few seconds passed, I noticed a blue glow coming from my hand. The circle patterns turned into hearts as they released blue magic that flowed into Jasper's hand. The dark, burnt spots disappeared as the lost, peeling scales grew back and healed.

I let go of Jasper's hand in disbelief as I remembered what Atom had said when we rid the giant turtles after escaping Pearl!

A wide grin came to my face and I shouted, *"Of course! That could help keep you alive until we reach the other side!"*

Jasper nodded, believing I was right.

Another explosion was heard from behind, and I turned to see another black cloud of smoke rise to the surface.

You will have to move quickly and avoid those bursts of smoke. The souls have told me that if you go into one of them, you'll never be seen again!

"Got it, Orla," I said as I held Jasper's hand again. "We must stick together and avoid those bursts of smoke in order to get to the other side!"

Lulu and Jasper both nodded. Then Jasper gestured to Lulu as he opened his mouth, allowing her to hide inside. She swam and wriggled in as he carefully closed his jaws over her.

We both took a deep breath.

Finally, we made our way through together.

The surrounding waters were really warm, which worried me about Jasper as he was extremely sensitive to high temperatures. So, I made sure that as long as he was close and holding my hand, letting my healing ability keep him alive, everything would be alright.

One or two explosions of black smoke erupted around us unpredictably from time to time. But as we progressed through the vents, more of them began erupting quicker than before, meaning we had to be extra careful and avoid the black smoke that rose to the surface.

At one point, we had a very close call, and Jasper got really burned on his leg and flipper, which was extremely damaged, and the web was torn. I could see the pain he was experiencing as he tried to resist and not spit out Lulu by accident. But he never let go of my hand, allowing my healing ability to recover his leg, making him feel much better.

The further we progressed, the harder it became as the vents erupted more and more frequently! We had to make sharp turns from left to right as we sped up and even dashed over a few of the black clouds before they covered us in their unavoidable heat.

The water got warmer, warmer and warmer until I felt like I was being boiled inside, and I started to slow down.

Jasper started pulling me with him as his body gained darkish spots nearly everywhere. His cheek fins were damaged, as were his scales and flippers, even as they tried to heal with my power.

Then, from the distance of the seamounts, we started seeing more mountains, free from hydrothermal vents and covered in corals and columnar jointing formations towering from the top.

Our eyes widened as relief filled us that we were nearing the other side of the vents.

You're almost there! Just keep pushing through! Orla cheered us on in our minds.

Excitement filled our bodies, and we swam faster.

But then, out of nowhere, a thermal vent from below erupted, and the black smoke hit Jasper's right arm and half of his belly, and something flew from his mouth

"*Jasper!*" I cried when I saw what had happened. I let go of his hand and checked if he was alright. He stopped swimming and clenched his right arm as his legs curled over his belly. He cried in agony, and then I noticed his mouth.

It wasn't glowing gold!

Fear struck me, and I exclaimed, "Where's Lulu?"

"*Charwie! Help!*" Lulu cried out from further ahead.

I turned as Jasper struggled to lift his head, and we saw Lulu waving her fins with a look of distress in her pink eyes.

Then we noticed from below her that a thermal vent was about to erupt and try to take her away.

"*Lulu! Hang on! I'm coming!*" I shouted.

I started swimming for her. But suddenly, Jasper nudged me out of the way, swimming faster than I was, straight to Lulu as the vent exploded, and black smoke rose below her.

He pushed her away, and the black smoke covered

him!

"*Jasper!*" I screamed! My heart raced, and my eyes grew wider than they ever had before!

I heard a high-pitched, panicked scream from the other side, and I knew that it was from Lulu.

When the black smoke began to clear and the vent below calmed, I could see Lulu's light, and I was glad she was alright. But I could also see Jasper's body had turned darker, and he began sinking to the ground. I quickly swam beside the vent, caught him in my arms, and made my way to the end of the thermal vents as Lulu followed me, her mouth covered by her tiny fins as her eyes filled with golden tears.

When we eventually reached the nearby columnar jointing formations on top of the underwater mountains, I carefully laid Jasper on the ground, his head over a soft coral.

He looked badly burnt; his scales were damaged and missing, his fins were burned, and his eyes were closed.

I cupped my hand over his cheek. "Jasper! Don't do this to me! C'mon, dude!" I trembled.

I placed my other hand on his chest as my stress grew so intense that I felt colder in the water.

Lulu came and tried placing her tiny fins on his face in front of me, hoping he would wake up with her light.

But no luck.

My hands clenched into fists and I pressed them over his body as I felt tears forming in my eyes, fearing that I might have lost a friend.

"No. Jasper! Don't do this to me! I'm serious! You

can't do this right now! I can't do this without you. I truly can't!" I sobbed as I pressed my head on his belly.

Lulu's golden tears slowly floated into the water as they solidified into golden pearls that rolled down from the basalt and into the deeper waters below.

The pressure in my hand that was on his chest was relieved and flattened over his heart.

But then, a moment later, I felt something gently grabbing my hand, and his chest started rising and falling deeply. I lifted my head and saw his hand was over mine as my hand released the glowing blue magic that was being absorbed into Jasper's body, repairing his damaged fins and scales, and growing new ones he had lost in the thermal vents.

My eyes widened, and my sadness faded away, turning into disbelief.

As the last of his burns disappeared, he slowly opened his eyes and lifted his head as he grinned. "I'm not going anywhere."

Wide smiles came onto our faces.

"Jasper! You're alive! I thought we lost you!" I wrapped my arms around him, giving him a tight squeeze.

He returned my hug as Lulu rubbed her body against his healthy cheek.

"I'm very relieved I am, thanks to you, Charlie," he replied.

We let go of each other, and I pressed my hands on his chest again, and said, "Don't do that ever again! You almost gave me a heart attack, even though I've said that before!"

He chuckled. "I risked my life to save hers, just like you said earlier."

"But...you were badly burned from the black smoke!"

"I may have, but that didn't stop me from saving her."

I sighed, knowing he was right with what he said. "Why should I be mad? I'm proud of you, Jasper. I really am." I grinned widely.

He risked his life to save hers! Orla said in my head.

Thank you for saving my life, Jasper! You're a hero! Lulu said telepathically.

"You're welcome, Lulu."

I glanced at the thermal vents we managed to get past and noticed the bright glimmers of his old scales as they slowly burned away, the glimmering fading away with them.

I felt Jasper trying to get up, so I moved off him so he could rise from the ground, kicking his flippers again. But then his eyes widened, and he pointed at something behind me. "Look!" he exclaimed.

Lulu and I both turned and saw glowing blue figures in the distance, swimming past the tall mountains in the same direction as we were.

They had the wings of Manta Rays and long, flexible antennae that stretched from their heads all the way past their pointed rears. Their eyes between their heads glowed a sky blue, and their pupils were the same colour as their fully bioluminescent skin.

The blue creatures left behind a glowing trail of

sparkling blue light as they made their way further in.

We had found the Manta Ray Sea Slugs!

We were all so excited to finally see the creatures we had searched so hard for.

"It's the Manta Ray Sea Slugs! We finally found them!" I exclaimed.

We all started waving our arms to try to catch their attention, even calling out to them.

"*Over here! Hey! We need you to take us to Orla!*" I shouted.

"*I want to go home!*" Lulu shouted.

"*Over here! Wait!*" Jasper shouted.

But the Manta Ray Sea Slugs just kept swimming until they disappeared into the mountains, possibly searching for remains.

There was a moment of silence as shock filled us that the Manta Ray Sea Slugs weren't interested in us.

"They're not interested in us! We cannot give up!" I exclaimed.

They aren't interested in you for a reason. They only search for the remains of any creature that has passed, Orla reminded us.

"I know, Orla! How are we gonna find the remains of a creature, or perhaps a leviathan by any chance?"

I tried to think, but my head started to hurt and my eyes became heavy. My shoulders slumped as I slowly sank toward the ground, my legs collapsing like jelly.

Jasper quickly caught me and must've sensed what I was feeling because he said, "You're tired from the thermal vents, Charlie. You need rest."

"But I can't. We made it all this way; I can't catch a

break right now," I replied softly, my fatigue getting the better of me.

You have plenty of time to find my servants, dear. Catch up on your slumber, Charlie. I believe there are a few caves nearby where you three may rest.

"Are you sure, Orla?" I asked, my eyes barely staying awake.

Truly positive, Charlie.

The water began to turn darker noticeably. I felt like I had no energy left after the thermal vents.

"I'll find us some shelter, Charlie. Just wrap your arms around my neck, and I'll carry you," Jasper said as he gently lifted me up and spun himself around for me to wrap my arms around his neck. He held my hands that lay over his chest and started swimming as Lulu followed him, beginning the search for a cave to call the night.

Chapter 20

The last Shelter

The water had turned dark, leaving the only lights being the corals, algae growth from the basalt formations, and scattered seagrass that waved in the gentle current.

Jasper searched from mountain to mountain for a cave as I held onto him.

Lulu was still awake, even though she would be asleep by now, but decided to stay up longer and help search with Jasper.

Sounds of thunder were heard from higher above as flashes of lightning struck the ocean's surface.

I watched as the lightning clapped and flashed. I thought it was cool to watch.

Usually, I'm not a huge fan of storms. But now and then, I like to watch them from far away if one is coming toward the Mainland. This, however, was something I had never experienced in my life as a goddess before!

I don't see that a lot of the time down from my Deep Spirit Tree, Orla said in my head.

I bet you don't because of how dark it was seeing it in my dreams, I thought.

Lulu must've heard my inner voice with her

telepathy when she asked Orla, *That was how you lost me…wasn't it?*

That was how I lost you, Lulu.

Why didn't you go after me, Mama?

I worried I would lose another one of your brothers or sisters. I had no choice but to call for help.

And I answered your call, Orla, which is good that I did, I thought.

It is true. You have come so far already! Once you finally reach my servants, they will take you to my Deep Spirit Tree, and we and Lulu will finally be a whole family once again!

Lulu and I smiled widely.

As soon as you know it, Orla. As soon as you know it!

I can't wait to go home!

I bet you can't, Lulu. You'll finally get to see your family!

Lulu giggled at me. But then quickly, her smile turned into a frown as she realised something. "Jayjay, Sandy and metal creature aren't here."

Frowns filled all our faces, and we missed our friends too.

"Even though we went far, we still haven't found each other yet," I said softly.

There was a pause for a moment.

Then Jasper spun his body around, causing me to let go. He held my hands as he kept swimming, and his smile returned. "Hey. We will find them eventually. They may still be out there; we need to stay strong and keep searching for them. Sooner, later or at any moment, we will find each other again…I promise. Let us not lose hope, Charlie, keep your spirits up," he comforted.

I smiled at him, knowing he was right. "You remind me of Chuckboi a little bit because you're so good at keeping up our spirits."

He chuckled as his heart started glowing, revealing it so slightly that you could almost see it pumping. "I'm glad you think so."

He then slowly tugged me closer as he spun his body again, and I wrapped my arms around his neck again, continuing the search for shelter.

Eventually, after a bit of time, we caught a glimpse of a blue light glowing inside a cave a bit further down to our left. Jasper immediately swam straight for it as I held on; Lulu followed close by us.

When we were in front of the cave, it turned out to be a large geode of tiny blue, glowing crystals on all surfaces with a big sponge coral cushioning the ground.

We went in, and I let go of Jasper as he sat down, gently pressing his hands on the coral to test its softness.

"This should do for the night," he said to himself.

I sat down on the coral. It felt so soft, like the pillows in the Den back in my ship, that I lay down, my arms under the side of my head, facing him.

"Man, this is the softest coral I've ever felt," I murmured to myself.

Jasper chuckled when he heard me. "It truly is,

Charlie. It's like the Seaflower back in my reef."

"Is that what that huge flower is with the long roots digging in and out of the sand?" I asked.

"It is. Jayjay sleeps inside of it while I sleep below it."

"That's… interesting. From earlier, back when we met the second time, I heard you say that it was *your* nest?"

He nodded. "Yeah. It's where me and Jayjay hang out most of the time. Do you mind if I pet your hair and hum you and Lulu a song?" he asked.

Lulu beamed as she swam onto Jasper's chest. His hand went over her, gently caressing her fragile body.

"Do whatever you want, Jasper, as long as it makes you happy," I answered.

He reached his hand out for my head, gently caressing my hair. I closed my eyes and enjoyed the feeling, as it also reminded me of Chuckboi comforting me when I felt down or just for a cuddle.

He started humming another beautiful lullaby of the sea, helping me and Lulu go to sleep faster.

I loved hearing his song so much because it made me feel safe.

I yawned in my sleep. "G'night, Jasper."

"Goodnight, Charlie," he whispered as he eventually moved his hand off my head and onto mine, which lay on the coral. I felt him lifting my hand and bringing it closer to his lips, and he planted a gentle kiss.

That made me open my eyes and stare at him. My

face heated up, and I felt baffled at the same time.

He noticed my expression, smiled, and said, "It's how I show how much I care about my friends. I do it to Jayjay all the time because she is my best friend."

Hearing that, my bewilderment faded away, and my face cooled down.

"Friends can also share their warmth and affection with each other, too," he added.

"Oh! I only thought you did it to fish because I was told it meant good luck," I said.

"Not always necessarily. I spread my affection to not only to Jayjay but to the rest of my reef, even visitors like the whale sharks," he answered.

"Well…thanks for sharing your affection," I said as I softly smiled.

"You're welcome," he replied. "Now, get some slumber, Charlie."

I closed my eyes again and yawned.

Jasper caressed my arm until he fell asleep.

We were so close to finally reaching the Manta Ray Sea Slugs! But the next morning, we'd have to find the dead body of any creature in order to get their attention and also hopefully find our friends.

Sandy and Atom? Where are you? I wondered. *I hope we will find each other again! If we ever do, where would we have met up? I hope that it will be around here or so. I just want to see you again!*

Chapter 21

Under the Seamounts

That night would have been one of the best nights for sleeping; I caught up on my sleep. The last few nights, I had slept on the whales and Xanaarhaah; their scales and skin were rough and hard as they were also on the move through the sea, making it feel very uncomfortable. The coral that we slept on was the softest one I had ever felt in days!

I woke as the sun's light burst through the water, illuminating everything.

I sat up and yawned, rubbing my eyes. "Morning."

Suddenly, something pressed against my lips, and I opened my eyes.

Lulu was covering my mouth with her tiny fins. "Ssh," she said, "Japper is still asleep."

Right, sorry, I thought as I slowly nodded.

I heard Orla's voice. *You're finally awake.*

Sorry! Did I disturb you?

Don't worry, you didn't, my dear. I told Jasper what I had told you in his dreams.

Do you mean about his ancestors and the special bond they made with you?

Yes. I thought it was time to tell him when he

fell asleep.

How did he react when you told him the history?

He was surprised by it all, and he told me he never knew any of it. After learning it all, he told me he still belongs to the reef. It is an understandable answer and decision he has made, and he has his own path to take and change.

Everyone does.

I glanced at Jasper, who was still asleep, his arms curled under his head like a pillow and his legs also tucked in.

I softly smiled at him until he moved one of his hands from under his head to rub his eyes as he stretched out his legs. Then he slowly sat up, stretched his arms and finally opened his eyes.

"Morning, Jasper," I said.

"Morning," he replied. "I had a crazy dream that I was in the Deep Spirit Tree with Orla."

"She told you about your ancestors' bond with her."

He turned his head to me sharply when I said that. "How do you know about that?"

"I've had it too, remember?"

"Oh yeah, I remember you telling me about that."

"It's inspiring to learn about your history of the tradition and the bond they have made with Orla."

"It is, actually. I never knew there was more of me in a place called Mersinganoid Cove, which was supposed to be my old home. But I was swept away and just couldn't remember anything because I was only a baby. It really hits you. But even now it hit me; I'm more happy in my reef," he replied.

"That's fair enough. You've lived on the reef your whole life, and you prefer to stick to it…just like coral."

He chuckled. "You know me too well, Charlie."

Suddenly, we heard Lulu gasp as she started rapidly moving around. She then spun around me as she laughed.

"What's wrong, Lulu? Why are you moving so quickly?" I asked, confused.

"I…I hear them!" she shouted.

"Hear who?" Jasper asked.

"Her! I hear them!" she shouted again as she squealed and even swam to Jasper's cheek fin and pulled it up.

He gently swept her off and asked again, "Who's 'her'?"

"Jayjay! Sandy! I hear them in my head!" she squealed.

Our eyes widened, and we gasped when she said that.

They must be nearby since she can now hear them again! Orla said happily.

We looked at each other as we began to smile, and I said, "Well, let's go find them if they are nearby!"

We swam out of the geode that had once kept us safe and started calling for our friends.

"*Sandy! Atom!*" I shouted.

"*Jayjay! Jayjay! Where are you?*" Jasper shouted.

We searched around the mountains as we called for them. We even searched further down as we continuously called for our friends.

Then we heard a voice nearby!

"Charlie! Is that you?"

It sounded like it was much further down the mountains. So, we descended until we were at the bottom and kept searching.

"Sandy! Atom! Where are you?" I called out, my excitement growing intensely.

We swam through narrow passes until we saw three familiar figures ahead, their hands cupped around their mouths, calling our names.

Our eyes widened excitedly as we recognised who they were!

"Sandy! Atom! Jayjay! We're over here!" I shouted.

They heard me, and they turned and saw us! Their jaws dropped, and Jayjay and Sandy squealed with happiness, so they swam straight to us. Atom laughed as he followed behind them.

We swam to them quickly until Sandy wrapped me and Atom in her wings and spun us around, laughing joyfully.

Jayjay wrapped all of her tentacles around Jasper, and he wrapped his around her body, pressing his head against hers.

"Charlie! Jasper! Thank Goddess, you guys are okay!" Atom said.

"I'm so glad you guys are okay! How did you find us?" I asked, still very happy to be reunited with Sandy and Atom again.

"Yeah! How did you?" Jasper agreed with my question.

Sandy showed a scale that seemed to belong to him.

"Back when we were in the glowing current! You lost one of your scales, and I caught it before we got separated!" Atom explained.

"It acted as our guide, and I took us all the way to you, thanks to my sense of smell and hindsight!" Sandy added.

"I discovered I have a defence mechanism!" Jayjay said.

Jasper gave her a very surprised look. "You have a defence mechanism?"

She nodded as she let go of him. "We ran into a lot of amazing sea creatures as we searched for you, even a swarm of Sea Monkeys that tried to steal our guide. We ended up in the mouth of a Leviathan, and I made it spit us out because I learned that I am toxic to taste!" she exclaimed.

Hearing that, Jasper smirked. "So that must have been why my lips keep swelling when I give you my friendly affection."

Jayjay placed her blue-tipped tentacles over her mouth as she giggled. "Sorry for that."

"No, don't be silly. I don't care if my lips keep getting swollen; you'll always be my best friend, Jayjay, toxic or not! I'm just so happy to see you again!" he said as he pressed his lips against Jayjay's cheek, his lips slowly swelling up.

Seeing his swollen lips, Lulu giggled as Sandy and Atom tried to hold back their laughter, and I snickered.

"Doesn't that burn or sting, Jasper?" I asked.

"It tingles for a little bit, but I don't care," he answered.

I laid my head on Sandy as Atom, and I were still wrapped in her wings, and Lulu joined us in the cuddle. We took deep breaths and let out sighs of joy now that we were back together.

"Now that we are thankfully back together, the only thing left to do is return Lulu to Orla. But first, we need to find a dead body somewhere in the mountains."

Sandy released me and Atom as they tilted their heads.

"Why?" Sandy asked, curious.

You aren't going to believe it, but we found the Manta Ray Sea Slugs last night! We tried to get their attention by shouting and waving our hands in the water, but they weren't interested in us, and Mama said that they only searched for dead bodies to bring to her, Lulu explained telepathically.

Sandy and Jayjay understood; however, Atom didn't know what was going on.

"Why are we all being silent? Is Lulu saying things telepathically?" he asked.

I repeated what Lulu had said to him, so now he understood.

"There has to be one somewhere, as Orla and Jasper said to me that we had plenty of time to search for one before they did," I said.

But then, we heard cracks from rocks above and another voice shouting angrily, "*Oh! The only dead bodies that they will find are yours!*"

We all looked up, and a large rock was falling down on us!

I quickly used my water powers to push Jasper,

Jayjay, Sandy, and Atom away. I grabbed Lulu and dashed backwards before the rock crushed us.

I looked up again with my eyebrows creased, and I saw another familiar figure appear from the blue, showing a really, really angry expression in their eyes. They showed their black razor-sharp teeth at me.

It was Pearl! She had found us, too!

"Why won't you all die!" she screamed as she smashed the rock she had latched herself onto so hard it was cracking.

"Not you again!" I shouted, breathing deeply after managing to escape and getting my friends out of danger just in time.

Pearl's face was as red as her tentacles, and her eyes were more orange as she continuously smashed the rock, with more cracks being heard and rocks from above beginning to break and fall down on us.

My friends swam over the rock and straight to me.

"You just don't know when to give up, do you?" she asked furiously.

"Here's a two-syllable answer for you: never!" Sandy shouted, giving an angry look back and showing her sharp teeth.

Lulu hid herself in my hands as I gently covered her.

Pearl could see her light and she said to us, "This is your last chance to surrender to me the fish. Surrender it to me now!"

I turned my body away but left my face turned to her.

"We will never give you Lulu, Pearl! If you want her

" Jayjay yelled.

We all agreed with her as they all went in front of me, defending me and Lulu.

I closed one of my fists and swung it out so that it turned into its bladed form, and I glared angrily at her.

But Pearl wasn't overwhelmed by our protest. "Fine! Have it your way as this will be *your last move!*"

She then scuttled down and roughly landed in front of us, her tentacles coiling and gripping hard onto the ground.

Jasper and Sandy hissed at her as his scales flared and his pupils constricted.

Pearl breathed roughly and yelled as she scuttled towards us, "*Here I come!*"

We quickly turned around and swam away as she chased after us further into the narrow passes.

Chapter 22

The hunter, the hunted and the rumbling

We swam through small tunnels, gaps, and even cracks within the walls. But Pearl managed to get through it all, though she had to swim over to reach us on some occasions.

Rocks from above fell, and we had to dodge left, right, up, and down. Pearl was able to grab a lot of the stones and tried throwing them at us to slow us down. But I was lucky to glance and see what she was doing. I used my water powers to create powerful currents to throw them right back at her, hitting her face and jaw, and a few of her teeth were knocked out.

When she felt the missing teeth in her gums, she grew angrier at us, so much so that she stretched her tentacles to the walls around her to tower over us and tried to grab one of us.

She managed to grab Jayjay, and she screamed in fear.

Jasper heard her. "Jayjay! I'm coming!" He quickly swam and grabbed the tentacle that held Jayjay and bit it, causing it to lose mobility and release her. He took Jayjay's tentacle, and she wrapped the others around him.

"Thank you, Jasper!" she said to him.

We went through multiple paths under the tall mountains until we were heading to an area with various paths to take. This gave me the idea that my friends could get to safety while I let Pearl chase me until I could find a way to shake her off. So I shouted, *"Scatter!"*

"Scatter? We are not losing you again!" Sandy exclaimed.

"Just trust me!" I shouted back as we neared the paths. I glanced at Lulu and told her to hold onto my swimmers. She did that, and I quickly turned my body so I was facing my friends and Pearl. I crossed my arms over each other, and I could feel bubbles forming in my hands.

Seeing what I was doing, all my friends' eyes widened, and Jasper shouted, "Charlie! Wait!"

I uncrossed my arms, creating currents that forced them into the opposite paths as Pearl was pushed against the wall.

When Lulu saw what I did, she used her telepathy to ask me, *What are you doing?*

Trust me! I know what I'm doing!

I know what she is doing, too! Just hold on, Lulu! I heard Orla's voice say in my head to Lulu.

I turned around again and kept swimming as Pearl chased after me and Lulu.

"You force your friends away, so it's just me and you and the fish! Now, this will be an interesting feast once I catch you!" Pearl bellowed.

"But catch me if you can, Kraken head!" I shouted as I blew a raspberry at her.

"*For the last time…I…am…not…a Kraken!*" She slammed her tentacles onto the walls repeatedly, causing more and more rocks to fracture and break off, falling on us.

"Oh shoot! Hang on, Lulu! I'll get us out of here!" I exclaimed.

Lulu whimpered as I moved one of my hands over, securing her in place as I kept swimming, eventually ending up in a big open area surrounded by narrow passes. I saw my friends leaving a few of them and stopped in the middle of the region as I did, too.

"Charlie! You didn't have to do that!" Sandy said.

"Do you still have Lulu?" Atom asked.

I showed them Lulu as she glanced at them. "Safe and sound."

"Not for long! Look out!" Jasper shouted as he pointed at Pearl from behind me.

I looked and saw she was about to tackle me because her tentacles were all out. She moved using all three of her back tentacles. I quickly used my water power to control the water around her when she leapt, and I threw her to the rock walls, hitting her head so hard against it that it cracked!

She fell onto the ground, sand rising in the water. She rubbed her head as it had flattened nearly above her eyes from the impact. She then held her breath to puff it back up and saw that the webbed fins on her head were damaged and ripped. When she felt it, her anger grew even more, and she went after us!

We swam up and around her as we attacked one at a time, biting, stabbing, punching, kicking, and even

Jayjay placing her tentacles onto Pearl's tongue through the gaps of her missing teeth, burning her mouth so that she stumbled backward, putting her tentacles on it.

It was finally my turn. I dashed toward Pearl with my bladed hand out and the other over Lulu and slashed at her skin.

"Gah!" she cried as she placed another one of her tentacles over the cut, her five eyes closed. When she opened them, they were more orangey-red now, and she bellowed, "That's *it!* I'm done with this nonsense!"

She stretched out all her tentacles, managing to catch all of my friends but me and Lulu, held them as they struggled to free themselves from her tight grip, and she threw them onto a rock wall against each other!

I gasped in horror as my friends sank on top of each other, moaning and grunting in pain.

My heart began to race as I faced Pearl again with a furious look, teeth and fists clenched. "You're gonna regret that!"

I charged at her, ramming my head against hers so that she was knocked back to another one of the rock walls harder than she had done to my friends. More fractures and cracks rose and stretched.

She pushed herself off the wall and tried whacking me with her tentacles. I managed to dodge all of them as they each slammed into the walls, leaving more and more cracks and fractures everywhere, and small rocks began falling on us.

When we noticed and looked up, more enormous

rocks began falling, and the ground began to shake.

I had to think of something quickly to keep my friends safe, so I looked around rapidly. When I looked up again, I saw a tunnel and thought it was a great place to protect them. So I let go of Lulu and used my water abilities to control the currents, lifting them to the tunnel, even Lulu, protecting her as well.

She tried swimming with me, but the current was too strong for her, so she was brought to my friends.

Charlie! What are you doing?

I smiled at her. *I'll be okay, Lulu, I promise. But I can't take you with me this time. It's too dangerous.*

Faintly, I saw my friends' eyes slightly open and watched me until they were put into the tunnel with Lulu, who was now screaming my name aloud now.

I used a larger rock that was falling from above to cover the entrance, protecting them from the falling rubble.

Pearl shook her head until her eyes met mine, followed by a menacing growl. "This…ends…*now!*"

I swam away as she chased after me once again through one of the passes.

I avoided all of her tentacles, as her movement was a bit slower and weaker that time, and also the rocks that fell in front of me that I had to swim over, and some I had to dash through before I was crushed.

That kept up for a few minutes until I was met with a dead end.

A dead end! It's too high to swim over! Orla stammered.

I sharply turned around, and Pearl blocked my

way.

"Finally!" she panted, "I have you now! Time to satisfy my hunger!"

My eyes widened, and my breathing quickened as I thought I was actually going to be eaten. I covered my face with both my arms and closed my eyes as Pearl charged right for me, her mouth wide with a few gaps of missing teeth!

But then, I felt massive vibrations from everywhere!

Thud! Bang! Crash! Crumble!

The sounds were so loud and hard that it was like explosions were heard from everywhere!

I curled my legs, and I sank to the ground, landing softly on my butt as I waited for the phenomenon to end.

When it was finally over, there was silence.

The water was so full of sand that I coughed. I waved my hands around, trying to get rid of the smell until it was gone.

Everything was darker.

Was I in Pearl's stomach?

What had happened?

Confused and scared at the same time, I opened my eyes, only to see that I was buried under large rocks that had fallen from above, covering me with a tiny bit of space. Luckily, there were a few gaps that I could fit through from my tiny form. So, I shrunk and swam through and grew back to my normal size.

From outside, larger rocks were stuck between the pass higher up and smaller rocks were in front of me, where Pearl was.

Speaking of Pearl, I wondered *where* she was.

Did she escape?

I swam forward until I noticed a glimmer from below. I swam down, all to see a big, black spade-drill-like tooth lying on the ground in front of the pile of rocks behind it. I picked it up and wondered, *How did it come out?*

You're alright! What happened? Orla asked in my head, who was also confused.

I took a few deep breaths as I was still trying to calm down and figure out what had happened.

"Pearl kept hitting and ramming into the slopes, causing the rocks to fall and collapse from the powerful vibrations. But I don't see her anywhere."

I faced the pile of rocks in front of me and decided to rummage through them until I saw a bit of red within. I moved and dug more rocks out of the way until I uncovered one of Pearl's tentacles!

Was Pearl…dead?

To check, I carefully lifted the tentacle and chucked it up to see if it would stay. But it sank back onto the ground, motionless. I picked it up again, turned one of my hands into its bladed form, and slowly cut it to see if Pearl would react to the pain.

But there was still nothing.

I was stunned when I realised she was actually dead! She was crushed by the rubble she had caused, and I was lucky to just get through the phenomenon.

I heard the voices of my friends calling my name from the opening where we once fought Pearl.

"*I'm over here!*" I shouted to them.

They heard me and came to me.

"Charlie! Oh, thank Mercy! You're okay! No scratches or booboos?" Sandy asked worriedly.

I didn't know what else to say as I was very shocked.

When they noticed my expression and Pearl's lifeless tentacle, they were at a loss for words, too.

Finally, Sandy asked, "Is Pearl…dead? Like 'dead' dead?"

Atom came to place both his metal white hands on the flesh to check for signs of life.

Eventually, his eyes widened even more, and his pupils shrank as he soon felt how I was. "No signs of life detected. She's actually gone!" he said.

Orla then said that she wasn't gone yet in me and Jasper's mind.

"What are you talking about, Orla?" I asked her.

She may seem lifeless, but her soul is still trapped inside. She needs to come to my Deep Spirit Tree. Now that her soul can't control her body anymore, my servants will arrive soon. She may have tried to eat my daughter and died; she doesn't deserve to die here. A tentacle will do enough to transport her soul.

I paused for a moment to take this all in. Finally, I agreed to do that. "As you wish, Orla."

I placed one hand on the tentacle and used my bladed hand to cut it off.

Jayjay, who was the closest to Lulu, covered her eyes and said to her just before I did so when she noticed what I was doing, "Don't look, Lulu."

She, Atom and Sandy were confused as to why I did that, so Jasper explained what Orla wanted me to do because she wasn't in their minds.

Then, we heard the sounds of clicking and calls from above, and we saw three Manta Ray Sea Slugs descend towards us to collect Pearl's remains.

Lulu gasped with delight, and she swam to me. We watched until they surrounded Lulu and me.

They were much bigger than I thought they were; they were twice my size!

They all stared at me as I was holding Pearl's tentacle.

I glanced at it for a moment, then I said to them, "Please take us and Pearl to Orla. We need to return Lulu, her daughter, back to her. We came all this way to find you and get your help for our last descent into the Twilight Zone."

They looked at each other for a moment, then their eyes met mine again and nodded to help.

Smiles filled our faces as they laid their backs flat onto the ground for us to climb on. Jasper, Lulu and I went on one, and Atom, Sandy, and Jayjay went on another, leaving the third empty.

They took us up from the seamounts, leaving Pearl's buried body behind as we brought one of her tentacles, containing her soul, with us.

After reaching the top, the Manta Ray Sea Slugs swam through the biome until we made it to the other side, where we were met with extremely deep waters that were just pitch black.

In the distance, a gold bright light shone, signalling

that we were almost there.

Lulu giggled happily when she saw her mother's bright light!

The Manta Ray Sea Slugs took us straight to it.

Chapter 23

The last dive

The Manta Ray Sea Slugs took us through the ocean's depths, where we saw a few Long-Finned Leviathans for the first time, along with Moonrays, schools of fish, and a pod of Blue-Spotted Whales further in the distance.

The Manta Ray Sea Slugs we rode on swam past the creatures until they dove down into the inky abyss below.

"Hold on, guys!" I said.

We all held on as we went further down until we started seeing small, vibrant and colourful lights twinkling in the abyss. They must've been the floating Sea Stars Orla used to mention because they twinkled and shone like the stars in space.

Welcome to the Twilight Zone, Orla said in my head.

"This place is beautiful!" Sandy said.

"It's so beautiful that I want to take pictures and study the lights and fauna!" Atom exclaimed.

"I don't think the creatures would like that," I said.

Atom thought that was fair, so he didn't.

Eventually, the bright gold light up ahead started getting clearer and clearer until it finally showed the branches and roots of the Deep Spirit Tree and the giant kraken, the Mother of Gold, aka Orla, who watched us as we approached.

When Lulu saw her for the first time, she squealed, "Mama!"

I could tell Orla was so happy to see the shining baby light that she said in my head telepathically, *My Golden Starpearl has come back to me!*

Sandy, Atom and Jayjay were so amazed by seeing her for the first time that their jaws dropped and their eyes widened.

"Is that her? She is huge!" Sandy exclaimed.

The Manta Ray Sea Slugs brought us close to Orla's giant eye as I held Pearl's tentacle.

Lulu immediately swam to her eye as Orla softly narrowed it until she pressed her head onto her for the first time.

I thought that was so heartwarming that I almost wanted to cry.

Then, from around Orla, the rest of her spawn must've heard Lulu's voice, and they swam to her. I was super happy she was reunited with her family again. They wrapped her around in their tentacles and bodies, and they giggled and purred.

When they all let go of her and Lulu swam away from Orla's eye so she could open it again, they all looked at me with positive expressions.

Thank you for bringing her back to me, little brave heroes.

"You're welcome, Orla," I replied with a nod.

Lulu swam back to me and Jasper with a big,

thankful smile.

"Here we are, Lulu. You're finally home!" I said softly.

She made a gesture by reaching her tiny fins out for my hand. I lifted it to her, and she held it.

Thank you all so much for helping me find my way home! she said to all of us telepathically.

We nodded.

Sandy placed her hand on Atom's head again to make him nod.

"I can't believe it, Lulu. This journey is finally over," I said.

Her expression changed, and she shook her head. *My journey is finished, but yours isn't done yet. Now, you need to go home, back to the shallows, where you all belong!*

We all looked at each other when she said that telepathically, and we believed she was right.

"You're right, Lulu! It's not over for us! We're gonna miss you, Lulu," I said, my voice almost cracking.

She swam up to my forehead and pressed hers against my Mindatar symbols.

I let go of Pearl's tentacle as it slowly sank to the roots below, where her soul would now live for eternity and be free from hunger.

I'm going to miss all of you! Maybe one day, when I learn to make dreams, you'll see me! Lulu said telepathically.

That made us feel much happier when she said that in our minds. We all knew we wouldn't be able to visit her again, but she could see us in our dreams one day when she got older and learned more abilities from her mum.

Lulu and I cuddled for a very long time, and my friends decided to join in, embracing the love Lulu shared with us.

When we eventually let go of her, Jasper and I heard Orla's voice again. *Dear Jasper. For having such a gentle and golden heart, I wanted to give you a blessing. Come closer, Jasper.*

Jasper swam a little closer as Orla lifted one of her giant tentacles in front of him. *Hold my tentacle.*

He glanced at her for a moment before he placed his hand on hers and stood there for a moment with his eyes closed. We then suddenly noticed gold patterns beginning to spread all around his arms and legs! Once they were all over his body, Orla spoke again in me and his mind.

You may let go now, Jasper.

He removed his hand from hers, opened his eyes, and noticed the new patterns all over his body. He turned and spun around in amazement. "What is this blessing you have given me, Orla?"

It is a blessing that eternally gives you freedom from being burned by the sun and heat ever again.

Beyond hearing this, his breathing quickened, and a huge smile crossed his face, and he started laughing. "Now I'll be able to explore the surface without ever getting burned again! Thank you so much, Orla!"

She softly chuckled. *I strongly believe you deserved it for having a heart of gold. Now, it is time that I return you all to the shallows, where you*

We all knew she was right.

Then, for one last time, we faced Lulu as she and her siblings waved goodbye.

We waved back, and I said to her, "See you one day in our dreams, Lulu."

She nodded.

Then, from all around me and my friends, gold magic circled, becoming brighter and stronger until we were so engulfed by it that we couldn't see Lulu, her siblings, Orla or the Deep Spirit Tree anymore.

Chapter 24

Back in the shallows

As the magic faded away, we found ourselves back in the reef, where it had all begun.

The sun's light burst through the crystal-clear water, and corals flourished as the creatures swam peacefully.

When they saw Jasper and Jayjay, they all beamed and swam straight to them, cuddling and rubbing their bodies against them, making them laugh.

"You've returned! Just like you said!" they exclaimed.

"Told you we would return!" he said as he laughed.

Atom, Sandy, and I laughed with them until we all calmed down and the sea creatures let them go. Some swam away while the rest stayed when they noticed his golden patterns. "What happened to your body, Whisperer?"

"I've been blessed by a giant, golden kraken that made a bond with my ancestors a long, long time ago," he answered.

Their eyes sparkled when they heard that, and they wanted to learn more about it. But Jasper said he would tell them later, so they all swam away, continuing with their everyday lives.

He and Jayjay took a deep breath.

"So good to be home," he said.

"I'm gonna miss Lulu," Jayjay said with a frown.

"Don't worry, Jayjay. She said that she would one day learn how to make dreams from Orla, and we'd see her when we slept," I reminded her.

Jayjay believed I was right and her smile was restored.

"That was a crazy, fun adventure. Though we got separated by Pearl, we found each other again and finally returned Lulu to where she belongs," Sandy said.

"I learned so much about sea life and flora. But since we are back, should we tell Kira about this?"

We paused for a moment.

Finally, me, Sandy and Atom answered at the same time as we laughed, "Naahh!"

We thought Kira would believe we had gone through the cenote, where Pearl used to stalk and once tried to catch her. So it was probably best not to tell her.

"Who's Kira?" Jasper asked, curious.

"She's a village chief who protects the village that lives close to our ship. Maybe one day, by overhearing that you can't burn anymore; you should visit!"

Jasper thought about that, then nodded. "Maybe one day, Sandy. Maybe one day. You can't really swim on the surface, can you?"

We shook our heads.

"No, you can't. But don't worry; I'll teach you how to walk and interact with people! You will love it; you'll get to experience what it's like and eventually tell Jayjay about it!" I said.

Jayjay nodded, beaming at what I said.

"Speaking of the surface, we should better get *back to the surface* and see our friends again, especially you, Atom, in your actual form," Sandy said.

"Good idea. I gotta collect the samples I have stored in here, so I can study them!" Atom said as he patted his metallic blue chest, containing the samples he had collected.

"That's not your actual form right now?" Jasper asked.

"Nope. This is called a drone. I use my goggles to control its movement and speech," he answered.

Jasper paused. "I'm so confused."

"You'll understand eventually, Jasper."

"We should return to the surface. It has been such a great pleasure having you on our team! Until we meet again!" Sandy said as she and Atom started swimming for the ship.

"*I'll catch up! Just give me one second!*" I shouted to them.

"*Okay!*" Sandy shouted back as they swam further away.

Then I turned back to Jasper with a huge smile. "Jasper?"

"Yeah?" he said.

I dashed over and wrapped my arms around him with my eyes closed. He was so surprised by my sudden movement that his arms spread out, and he looked at me with wide eyes.

"Thank you," I said.

"For what?" he asked.

"For being there for me, to comfort me and sing to me."

I felt his arms and legs wrap around me as he pressed his head above mine when I told him that.

From under my eyelids, I could slightly see the pink glow of Jasper's heart and the golden patterns Orla had blessed him with shining brighter.

"You're welcome, Charlie," he said.

Jayjay joined in the cuddle.

Eventually, we let go of each other, and I waved to them before catching up to Sandy and Atom, who must have reached the surface and were waiting for me.

They waved back as I made my way through the reef, the Kelp Forest and finally back to the Alphanian Ship.

I was so happy to see it again after days of being out in the deep ocean, where I had learned so many things from Orla.

From near the shoreline, I could see faint figures of Sandy, Atom in his actual form at that time, holding his drone, and Chuckboi!

They must've noticed me from under the water as they started making gestures for me to come up to the surface.

I took a deep breath and turned to the Kelp Forest, where we had once searched for Lulu and met Jasper, for one last time.

Then I finally swam to the surface. My head rose out of the water, and I saw my three friends.

"There's my little Marshmallow!" Chuckboi said, so happy to see me again his eyes were pink.

I smiled widely as my heart began racing. Then, I used my water powers to control the water so that it put me onto the grass before splashing down and washing back into the ocean.

I tried to walk to Chuckboi, but just when I tried to take a step, I lost my balance and fell onto the ground. "Oof!"

"Oh, goddess! You alright?" Sandy asked.

"I'm fine, Sandy. Just still not used to walking in flippers," I replied as I tried to get up. I felt a bit heavy because of the water I was carrying on my body.

Thankfully, Atom and Chuckboi came and helped me up.

"Thanks, boys," I said.

"Anytime!" Atom replied. "Happy we're back on the surface?"

"Very happy…and cold."

Chuckboi then lifted me and held me in his arms. "Then let's get you warmed up and dry."

He started walking to the ladder that led up to the shipyard, and Atom and Sandy followed him. He let them climb up first, even putting me down so I could climb up with them as he joined us last.

We walked down the stairs as Chuckboi continued carrying me through the hallway, where a few of my friends were so happy to see me and Sandy that they gave her hugs. They gave me and Chuckboi space so I could be taken to my art room.

Chuckboi sat me down on my chair as he went to

the Den to grab a blanket. He then returned to me and wrapped me in it.

"Is that better, little Marshmallow?" he asked softly.

I nodded as I began to feel dry, and the blue patterns and bioluminescence disappeared, and I turned back to normal. My hair changed back, and my eyes weren't glowing blue anymore.

Chuckboi placed his arms between my shoulders and leaned forward to plant a kiss on my forehead. "I missed you, Charlie."

My face turned pink. "I missed you too, Chuckboi."

"I watched a lot of the journey through Atom's screen on his large computer thingy. His goggles also paired with it and allowed me to see through the drone's eyes. It surely looked like a lot happened. You even got separated by…'Pearl'?"

"Yes, we did get separated in the currents by Pearl, but we managed to find each other again. If you probably also noticed, the Mersinganoid, Jasper, his name is, was super sweet and took great care of me and Orla's daughter. He reminded me of you because he was so encouraging, and also, he had a heart of gold."

He chuckled. "Did he? Well, I'm glad he reminded you of me. What else happened with you, him and Orla's daughter?"

"We made our way through a place called the Gloom Forest, where we had to hide and escape Pearl, then rode on whales, encountered a Colossal Twilight Shark and even went through hydrothermal vents!"

His eyes widened. "And you managed to survive?

That's crazy!"

"Jasper was severely burned, though. But thanks to my regenerative powers, a shared symbolism of the Kyanite Wisp, I made him feel much better."

"Well, you're incredible like that, little Marshmallow. You always inspire me with your magic and bravery," he said.

I chuckled at his compliment.

Then Chuckboi replied, "Also, I think Atom has collected a lot of samples from *their* adventure. I might have a look later on."

"I also wanna see what he has collected too! Maybe after I get back into my diamond armour and once I'm warmed up enough. For now, I'm just gonna… chill," I said with a giggle as I shuffled my shoulders.

Chuckboi laughed at my joke. "See? I laugh at your jokes, even if some people say they were terrible."

"I would say the exact same thing if I was holding a piece of paper that said 'my jokes'. I would rip it in half and then say it was tearable."

We both laughed.

Atom, from his lab, who must've been sorting out the samples he had collected to study, overheard my joke, laughed too, and shouted, "*I can definitely agree, Charlie!*"

When we eventually calmed down, Chuckboi then said to me, "I'm gonna check out what Atom found. Alright if I leave you alone for now?"

"I'll be fine, Chuckboi," I said, smiling at him.

He smiled back, then left my room for Atom's lab.

I took a deep breath and turned to the small glass

window beside my art desk higher up. I got up and walked to it to watch the ocean horizon as I remembered the crazy and fun journey we had returning Lulu to where she belonged.

Then faintly, I noticed a small gold light from the far distance, growing brighter, as if Orla and her children were trying to catch our attention.

I smiled as I was happy for Lulu to be reunited with her family.

I was also honestly happy for Pearl. Even though she was a flesh-and-light-hungry lunatic, I believed she was feeling much better now that she was free from her starvation.

Then I noticed from further down the horizon that Jasper and Jayjay protruded from the water as if the light had also caught their attention.

They stared at it for a long time until the light faded away. They then looked at each other, chuckling, until they noticed my ship from further behind them.

They must've noticed me because they started waving.

I waved back until they dove into the water, Jasper's flippers kicking the air.

I was really happy for Jasper, now that Orla blessed him to have the freedom to explore the surface without ever getting burned by the sun again. He always wanted to explore the surface, and I thought maybe one day I could help him learn to walk and show him around.

He would've loved that!

After they had splashed back into the water, I

decided to go to Atom's lab and see what he had found. So, I turned around and headed there to see for myself.

Epilogue

The Deep Spirit Tree

Back in the Twilight Zone in the Deep Spirit Tree, Pearl's tentacle had reached the giant roots that dug deep into the seabed below.

The Manta Ray Sea Slugs had already made their way back into the open ocean, searching for more dead bodies to bring to Orla.

White smoke began covering the tentacle until it rose up to the branches as they cleansed the new coming soul from negativity it had, absorbing it and allowing the branches to grow slightly.

Orla, Lulu, and her siblings noticed, and Lulu watched in amazement until the soul was brought in front of them.

The white smoke began to take the form of Pearl as one of her tentacles was placed onto her ghostly head, and her glowing yellow eyes and white pupils were closed. Her lost eye had come back and her body was free from the wounds she had received from the fight back in the seamounts.

"Oh, my head. Why don't I feel hungry anymore?" she asked herself, confused as to why she was feeling full.

Because, my dear Pearl, you are dead, Orla said telepathically in Pearl's mind.

Pearl opened her eyes and met hers, and she

gasped in fright, but soon she felt a sense of safety filling her non-physical body.

She saw Lulu as she hid behind her siblings. But she didn't show any sign of aggression towards her, and was instead confused as to why she was scared. Then quickly, she realised. *"I tried to eat you, didn't I, Lulu?"*

Lulu was so confused when Pearl called her by her name that she slowly emerged from her siblings and swam to her.

You called me by my name. You did try to eat me. Are…you okay, Pearl?

"I'm…so sorry. When I get very hungry, I lose my mind and become very irrational and violent. I couldn't control myself at all and even tried to eat the Goddess and your friends who guided you to where you belong. I deserve to be stopped for being a big shrimp."

But you are safe now, Pearl. You will not be a ghost forever. The souls here are sometimes sent either to the sky, surface, or back in the water, reincarnating as either the same animal or a different one. Even as they do, my tree will still grow as new souls are brought to me. This is salvation for everyone who is brought here, even the largest of predators and the people I have made a bond with many, many years ago, waiting to be reincarnated. One day, it will be you, dear Pearl.

Her six eyes widened when Orla told her that. *"I can return to the land of the living?"*

One day. For now, your soul may live in peace, free from your hunger.

Pearl smiled, happy she was free from her hunger. Then she lowered her head and closed her eyes. "Thank you for bringing me here. If I ever reincarnate as something else and find any of Lulu's friends back in the reef, I want to tell them that I'm sorry for how I had behaved mindlessly towards them. I don't expect to be forgiven immediately, but that's all I want to tell them one day if I do. I promise that I will do better next time and follow nature's rules if they ever change in my next life."

THE END

IMAGINE: High Worlds

COMING SOON

THE SERIES

IMAGINE:

Book 1 - Imagine: a Wild Civilisation
Book 2 - parts 1, 2 and 3: Imagine: The Long Winter
Book 3 – Imagine the Golden Starpearl
Book 4 - Imagine: High Worlds
Book 5 - Imagine: A Dark Underworld

Book 6 - Imagine: The Rise of the Mindatar

...

www.ingramcontent.com/pod-product-compliance
Lightning Source LLC
Chambersburg PA
CBHW071424200726

48294CB00002B/512